"You wanted time . . ." ping the last piece of candy into her mouth. "I gave it to you."

How easily she could let herself believe that he was still in love with her, Carly thought. "Well, maybe you shouldn't have." She reached out, trailing her finger over the planes of his face. For a moment it was easy to forget he wasn't here anymore. "You never had any trouble telling me when I was wrong. Why didn't you?"

Dex caught her hand and held it for a moment. They gazed into each other's eyes and Carly knew that he was about to kiss her. Should she permit it? Her date was off ogling someone else . . . but it wouldn't be right.

Dex moved closer and she sighed, wondering where she'd find the strength to stop him. She wanted him to kiss her . . . *ached* for him to kiss her, and she could see by the look on his face that he intended to kiss her.

He lowered his head, his lips only inches from hers. "Carly, there's something I've been wanting to do all day," he said softly.

She gazed up at him, her eyes growing warm and liquid. How could she prevent him from kissing her when she wanted it as much as he did? Wrapping her arms around his neck, she murmured, "All right. Do it."

He calmly plucked a stick out of her unruly hair. "You've had this stuck in your hair for hours. . . ."

WHAT ARE *LOVESWEPT* ROMANCES?

They are stories of true romance and touching emotion. We believe those two very important ingredients are constants in our highly sensual and very believable stories in the *LOVESWEPT* line. Our goal is to give you, the reader, stories of consistently high quality that may sometimes make you laugh, sometimes make you cry, but are always fresh and creative and contain many delightful surprises within their pages.

Most romance fans read an enormous number of books. Those they truly love, they keep. Others may be traded with friends and soon forgotten. We hope that each *LOVESWEPT* romance will be a treasure—a "keeper." We will always try to publish

LOVE STORIES YOU'LL NEVER FORGET
BY AUTHORS YOU'LL ALWAYS REMEMBER

The Editors

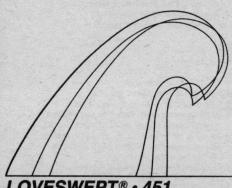

LOVESWEPT® • 451

Lori Copeland
Squeeze Play

BANTAM BOOKS
NEW YORK • TORONTO • LONDON • SYDNEY • AUCKLAND

SQUEEZE PLAY

A Bantam Book / January 1991

LOVESWEPT® and the wave device are registered
trademarks of Bantam Books, a division of
Bantam Doubleday Dell Publishing Group, Inc.
Registered in U.S. Patent
and Trademark Office and elsewhere.

If you would be interested in receiving protective vinyl
covers for your Loveswept books, please write to this
address for information:

Loveswept
Bantam Books
P. O. Box 985
Hicksville, NY 11802

ISBN 0-553-44086-1

Published simultaneously in the United States and Canada

PRINTED IN THE UNITED STATES OF AMERICA

OPM   0 9 8 7 6 5 4 3 2 1

One

Another Monday morning. A chance for new beginnings. And the start of her fourth diet this month.

It wasn't nine o'clock yet, and already Carly Winters was so hungry she felt as if she could gnaw a leg off a chair. There was a fierce look in her eyes as she strode toward her office.

"Morning, Carly."

"Morning, Janis," Carly called over her shoulder as she strode down the hallway.

"Hey!" Janis stood up from behind the reception desk.

"Have you heard who they've hired for the new marketing director . . ."

Janis's voice trailed off as she saw the hem of Carly's skirt disappear around the corner.

"Guess not." Shrugging, Janis sat back down. Reaching for her half-eaten chocolate-iced torpedo, she took a bite, licked the sinful stickiness off her fingers, then pressed down on one of the brightly flashing amber buttons. "Good morning, Montrose Research."

Down the hall, Carly sailed toward the board-room, trying to balance a cup of coffee—black no sugar—in one hand and a stack of folders in the other.

"Oops! Hey, watch it!" one of the mailmen said, nimbly stepping out of Carly's oncoming path.

"Sorry." Carly grabbed for a legal pad that was sliding down her hip and kept going.

The boardroom was filled when Carly walked in a moment later. Dropping her folders onto the table, she gratefully sank onto a padded leather seat next to David Honeycutt's chair.

"Hey, you're improving." He checked his watch. "Nine on the dot."

"Yeah, but it took concentration," Carly said.

"Doughnut?" David pushed the bulging tray closer to her.

She winced. "No thanks. I'm not hungry. Not very anyway." The bowl of oat bran she'd had for breakfast lay in her stomach like a rock.

"Oh?" David's eyes held an appraising look. She was sure his astute gaze had zeroed in on the extra pounds she'd gained over the weekend. "Coffee? Low-cal sweetener?"

"No, thank you," she returned coolly. "I have some." Or she had had a minute before. Now half of the contents from her cup were dotting the front of her blouse. At least she had resisted the temptation to add cream—even though the jar was clearly marked "light."

David casually opened his folder and slanted a wry smile in Carly's direction. He could be such a jerk when he tried. "Guess the new man arrives today."

"Oh? I hadn't heard."

Easing the heaping plate of pastry closer to himself, David made a show of trying to decide on one. "No kidding? Where have you been for the last couple of days? On a desert island?"

"In Detroit on business, why?"

David selected a plump Danish coated with a heavy layer of caramel.

Carly could feel herself beginning to salivate as he lifted the pastry to his mouth and took a big bite. He lifted his brows apologetically. "You don't mind, do you? I need a little pick-me-up."

Carly would have liked nothing better than to give him one. Straight through the ceiling. "No, go right ahead. I'll just eat my fruit."

She rummaged inside her purse for an orange and then began to peel it, wishing that it were David's pointed little head. "Who'd they hire?" she said, trying to be polite.

David lifted his brows again, indicating that his mouth was full.

"For marketing," she said. "Who'd they hire?"

Not that Carly planned to quibble over their choice. At this point, she'd take anyone she could get. She needed the help. As head of research and development, she was up to her ears in surveys.

Though she was a hard worker, twelve-hour days were not her idea of a job. She considered them a personal offense.

"Are you serious? You really don't know?"

"No, David, I really don't know," Carly conceded, "but whoever it is had better be able to hit the ground running because he or she is already buried up to their eyeballs in work."

Carly glanced up to see Martin Montrose enter the room. She was about to send him a good-morning smile when the room seemed to heave. A high-pitched ringing started in her ears as she gripped the edge of the table, suddenly feeling faint. Accompanying the president of Montrose Research was Dex Matthews.

Her *ex*-fiancé, Dex Matthews.

"Good morning, ladies and gentlemen." Martin smiled fondly at the assembled group.

Good Lord, Carly thought. Dex! What's he doing here? He'd left the firm a year before to take a position with a large advertising firm in San Jose. She wondered why he'd come back.

Dex's gaze immediately held hers. She could feel the pulse in her throat begin a slow, painful hammering. It had been a year, but he looked exactly the same. And he still had the power to affect her.

She lowered her eyes, noticing his Italian loafers and dark suit that was stylish but not trendy. The jacket was open, revealing a light blue shirt, a darker silk tie, a lean waist, and a long, muscular torso. He was clean-shaven, and was still too handsome for his own good. Carly had the sinking feeling that her life was about to be turned upside down, shaken like a feather duster.

Several of the men rose to their feet, shook Dex's hand, and exchanged brief pleasantries.

When the flurry of excitement died away, Dex walked around the table and took the empty seat next to Carly. "Long time no see," he murmured as he adjusted his chair.

"Yeah . . . how you doin'?" Carly almost groaned. Boy, that sounded incredibly stupid after what they'd once meant to each other. But, she guessed it wasn't the worst thing for someone who'd just been broadsided.

"What are you doing here?" she finally managed to say.

His smile was cool and a little distant. "It's a surprise."

"Well." Martin's smile was benevolent as his gaze traveled around the table. "We're all looking bright-eyed and bushy-tailed this morning." His lighthearted observation was met with the proper number of appreciative chuckles.

"I'll begin by saying how delighted I am with the firm's second quarter. After seeing the figures—"

Carly pasted a smile on her face, trying to follow her boss's comments, but she was incredibly aware of Dex sitting beside her. The familiar scent of Gianfranco Ferré drifted to her, and a warm curl twisted in her empty stomach.

What is he doing back? Her mind raced as memories blotted out Martin's voice. She had met

Dex at a meeting very similar to this one, over eight years before. They had been hired at about the same time. Back then both had been young, idealistic, and full of themselves. For years they'd worked together without ever really noticing each other. Carly had thought Dex was too brash, and Dex had considered Carly a little squirrelly. It was still a mystery to Carly how one day they'd both looked up and thought at the same time: Whoa! Where have you been all my life?

Maybe there was something to the old adage that opposites attract. Carly knew that she and Dex were about as opposite as two people could be, yet the attraction was suddenly there, lusty and virtually impossible to ignore.

They had been working in account services at the time. Dex was a planner, methodical and always in control. Carly was spontaneous and aggressive. Ideas flowed ceaselessly from her mind, and she couldn't act fast enough on a concept that excited her.

Even though their styles were different, both were good at their work. But their different approaches did cause problems. Since Dex thought things through and Carly acted impulsively, the two diverse personalities mixed like oil and water.

After months of working together Carly began to accuse Dex of being too critical, and Dex started telling Carly that she was a real kneejerk.

A kneejerk! That particular opinion still made Carly see red. Yes, she was impetuous, enthusiastic, and even passionate about her work.

But she was *not* a kneejerk.

"Well, I suppose it's time that we get down to the business at hand," Martin was saying.

Carly straightened, reaching for her cup of coffee. Dex's role here did not concern her. What they had was over. She had spent the last year convincing herself of that.

Martin's attention focused on Dex, his smile mirroring his admiration for the man. "Most of you know why we're here this morning. The Powder Puff Corporation has chosen Montrose to do the research for their new line of hygiene products. As a result," Martin continued, "we'll be working fast and furiously to prepare a comprehensive marketing plan based on the research we will be conducting."

Martin turned to Carly. "Most of you know Dex Matthews," Martin said. "Dex was associated with the firm for seven years before accepting a position with one of our rivals in San Jose last year. Miraculously, he has come to his senses and decided to rejoin Montrose."

A few uneasy chuckles sounded around the table, but Dex took the ribbing good-naturedly.

"Well, what can I say? A man can stand only so much of that California sunshine," he joked in his familiar way.

"Well, whatever has brought you back to Chicago, we heartily welcome your decision. Ladies and gentlemen, I present to you our new director of marketing, Dex Matthews."

The group welcomed this announcement with

vigorous hand-clapping, and after watching daz-
edly for a moment, Carly half-heartedly joined in.

With a feeling of déjà-vu, she sighed as the sig-
nificance of Martin's announcement sank in. If
Dex was their new marketing director, that
meant that they would be working together on
the Powder Puff account.

Carly's spirits sank lower as Martin continued
to sing Dex's praises. "For the one or two of you
in the room who have not met Dex, let me boast
a little. Dex came to us straight out of school,
having earned a master's degree in marketing.
I'm happy to say that his career began right here
at Montrose."

When he glanced at Carly, she closed her eyes.
She prayed he wouldn't mention her former
engagement to Dex.

"Unfortunately, the Simons Group wooed him
away from us and he was placed in charge of
developing marketing strategy there. You recall the
highly successful advertising campaign for Jolly
Good Peanut Butter?" Martin prompted. "And the
Summer Sippin' Lemonade campaign?"

Dex was given another round of applause.

Carly propped an elbow on the table, her chin
on the palm of her hand, and absently doodled
on her notepad. She wondered how the great and
mighty Dex Matthews was going to use his background in peanut butter and lemonade to peddle
hygiene products.

"Those, and other well-known campaigns, were
developed under Dex's direction as account

supervisor with Simons. And may I add," Martin said, concluding, "that he's just a dissertation short of his doctorate. I'm sure many of you have read his article this month in *Forbes* concerning present marketing strategy—if you haven't, then you'll want to purchase a copy on your way home."

Sure thing, Martin. Wouldn't want to miss it.

As applause broke out again, Dex leaned over and whispered to Carly, "You don't look impressed."

"Maybe because I'm not."

Dex grinned to himself, but there was no genuine warmth in the expression. His thoughts centered around Carly and the challenge she still inspired in him. Pretty soon she would be impressed with him. He'd make sure of it. After all, he hadn't moved back to Chicago because he was tired of sunshine and oranges.

When the applause died away, Dex stood up, smiling at the group. "Thank you, Martin, for the warm welcome. It's nice to be back. Now, if you'll look at the background material provided by Powder Puff, you'll see that they have done some preliminary work on the market they hope to reach." He paused, opening his folder. "But I can see right now we can do better."

The muscle in Carly's jaw tightened. She knew it. He was already criticizing her work. She'd done that preliminary study herself, and she'd told her contact with Powder Puff that he wasn't providing enough direction, but he had sworn that he was unable to pry more out of the mother company.

"I believe that with a little more probing we can come up with additional public response, hopefully giving us a better direction for the initial marketing strategy. Carly, I understand that you and I will be working closely on the project?"

Carly nodded.

"Then I want your group to begin developing a preliminary list of questions for a public opinion survey and a list of potential names for the product. We'll go over any problems you have on a daily basis."

Carly nodded again, refusing to meet his eyes, staring instead at his hands. He still wore the gold college ring with the blue stone. There wasn't a wedding band, though, and she wondered why she should feel so relieved.

After all, she had been the one who'd broken their engagement, not Dex—although, at the time, he'd been damnably passive about it.

Dex moved methodically through the material in the folder while Carly tried to focus her attention on what he was saying. After a while she gave up.

She hadn't seen him in over a year, and yet to her dismay she hadn't forgotten one single thing about him. Not one.

The tilt of his head, how his blue eyes darkened when he was engrossed in his work, the tone of his voice, the lively flash of his smile . . .

Carly, you're in trouble.

"So, if there are no further questions," Dex's gaze swept the table before bringing his part to a close, "I'll turn the meeting back to you, Martin."

"I have nothing more." Martin stood and shook hands with Dex again. Turning back to the group, he smiled. "Meeting adjourned."

The room filled with noisy chatter as the meeting broke up.

Carly quickly gathered her notes and darted for the nearest exit. Her heart sank as she saw Greta, the firm's most glamorous secretary, waiting for her in the hallway.

"Lucky you."

Carly paused, pretending to rearrange her folders. "Lucky me?"

"Yes, want to trade places?"

"If we can arrange it," Carly said lightly. She tried to edge her way out of the room, but Greta fell into step beside her.

"Are you serious? You're not thrilled about working with Dex Matthews?"

Thrilled? No. *Appalled* might come closer.

Dredging up her most optimistic smile, Carly forced herself to sound convincing. "Who wouldn't be delighted to work with a man who is so notable in his field?"

Carly could see that Greta didn't believe her.

"Oh—then you're not thrilled about working with him again."

"Not exactly."

"There aren't still hard feelings between the two of you, are there?"

Carly laughed. "Of course not." She hoped her casual, professional attitude would deflect any gossip Greta might be stirring up.

The oh-boy-since-you-don't-want-him-can-I-have-him look that had suddenly invaded Greta's eyes annoyed her.

She wished she thought Greta was good-looking and stupid, but that wasn't true. Greta was not only good-looking and intelligent, she had a body that men salivated over.

Luckily, one of the new hires—officially known around the hallowed halls of Montrose as administrative assistants—required Greta's attention.

Breathing a sigh of relief, Carly headed straight for her office before she could be interrupted again.

Dumping the folders on her desk, she dropped onto her chair, still smarting over Martin's lack of sensitivity.

Her gaze fell on the Powder Puff folder, and she leaned over to shove it beneath a pile of other work that she told herself had first priority.

A tap sounded at the door, and she glanced up to find Janis standing in the doorway, holding a large, colorful balloon bouquet.

"Guess who this is for?" she said in a singsong tone.

Carly's face brightened. "Me?"

"Who else gets flowers and balloons in this pit of overworked peons?"

Carly grinned as she accepted the gigantic helium-filled bouquet. "I suppose you already know who it's from?" There were no secrets around Montrose.

Janis smiled. "Naturally. 'One month today, Hayden,' " she quoted.

Carly shook her head, removing the card to read it for herself. "That's sweet."

"The man's got the hots for you."

"No, he doesn't, Janis. Hayden and I are just friends."

Janis's comical, round face looked skeptical. "Oh? Well, then why don't I get balloon bouquets from prominent corporate attorneys?"

"You don't have any prominent corporate attorney friends."

"I would if I got the chance."

Carly laughed, tying the bouquet to one limb of the coat rack. "I'll put a bug in Hayden's ear."

Janis stepped closer to the desk, her gaze searching Carly's anxiously. "I guess you know by now who they've hired as the new marketing director?" she asked in a lowered voice.

Carly's face remained expressionless. "I guess I do."

Janis edged nearer. "What do you think?"

Janis had left the door open so Carly could hear Dex's voice in the reception area. He was talking to the pretty receptionist Melody Evans, and their laughter was floating down the hallway.

Stepping to the door, Carly shut it. Loudly.

"All that racket," she grumbled. "How's a person expected to work with that going on—now, what was your question, Janis?"

Janis figured her question had just been answered.

Dex Matthews was back in town, and Carly Winters wasn't exactly doing handsprings.

Two

When the door closed behind Janis, Carly turned her attention to the computer terminal. She was annoyed to hear a tap on the door. Another interruption.

"Yes?" she called more sharply than she'd intended.

Dex's head popped around the corner. "Got a minute?"

Carly wished she could say no. Since he hadn't bothered to call or contact her during the past year, she didn't want to give him a morsel of her time. But her job required that she talk to him. "Sure, what's up?"

Dex glanced at the bouquet of balloons as he stepped inside the room. "You dating a clown now?"

She smiled, folding her hands on her desk

patiently. She could see that he was waiting for her reply, but she had no intention of making one.

"Something I can do for you?"

Sauntering casually over to the balloon bouquet, he studied the colorful spheres.

"Well?" she prompted him.

"Well, what?"

"Is there something you needed?"

A small smile touched the corners of his mouth as he casually removed the card and read the signature. "Hayden Winkler?"

"That's right."

He slid the card back into the envelope, then seated himself. "Hayden Winkler? What type of name is that?"

Oh, so this was how it was to be.

"Hayden isn't any concern of yours," she told Dex.

He shrugged. "True. I don't suppose anything about Hayden Winkler is likely to concern me."

Carly found that remark particularly unwarranted—and painful. He didn't need to remind her that the past year had been more hellish for her than for him. It still stung to remember how utterly calm he had been the night they had broken up. Later she had bawled her eyes out, agonizing over the decision. But when she'd told him, he had simply sat and stared at her as if she had gone off the deep end.

"Dex, I'm busy. Did you want something in particular? Something associated with the account?" she asked again.

She wasn't being cordial, but she felt sure that under the circumstances, he would understand. They might be forced to work together on the Powder Puff account, but she didn't plan to sit around with her feet on the desk, chit-chatting over trivialities with him.

His gaze met hers, and Carly felt her pulse start up that uneven *thurumpt* again. "Do I detect a hint of friction between us?"

"No," she began cautiously, "it's just that I think someone should have warned—told me you were returning to the firm."

"Oh?"

"Yes."

"And why's that?"

"Why? Well . . . because . . . someone just should have. Martin should have told me."

He smiled, and suddenly the tension drained out of her. Maybe this wouldn't be an impossible situation after all.

"Don't blame Martin," he said. "I didn't decide to accept the position until late last week. Martin wanted to tell you right away, but I asked him not to."

Carly frowned. "Why?"

"I wanted to surprise you."

She made a face. "It worked."

He grinned this time, and her heart did a crazy, completely irrational somersault.

Damn him, she thought. He still had the ability to charm a mouse out of a cat's mouth.

"Actually, I didn't want you worrying about it. I knew you might be uncomfortable with the situation, but I figured we're both adult enough to handle it," he said easily.

"That's what you figured, huh?" Her direct gaze told him that she wasn't quite sure she believed him.

"Don't you?"

She smiled, the faintest hint of warmth touching her eyes. "I suppose so."

"Your enthusiasm takes my breath away."

They both smiled this time.

"Okay, Matthews, so stop wasting my time. What do you want?"

"I just stopped by to make sure that we're not going to have a problem working together."

"I can get along if you can."

"I can get along." His eyes traveled over her leisurely, pausing occasionally to linger here and there. "I see no reason for our past differences to stand in the way of our jobs."

"I don't recall an instance when they ever have."

"And I don't want there to be one." His voice lowered persuasively, efficiently tying her stomach in a perfect knot. "We each have our separate interests now, but I see no reason why we can't be friends."

Our separate interests? Did that mean he was involved with someone?

"I see no reason why you and I can't be friends. Do you?" he prompted her.

Their eyes met, and Carly told herself to calm down. This wasn't so bad. She could look him straight in the eye and not burst out crying. "Sure, why not?"

"Good. I think that shows real growth."

Carly smiled lamely. Yeah, real growth.

"And you've been okay?" The sudden concern that came into his voice caught her off guard.

"Great. And you?"

"Great."

"I'm surprised you asked."

Had she said that!? Please, she hadn't, had she?

His brow lifted. "Pardon?"

"I'm surprised you asked." She'd said it again! "Why?"

"Because it's been a year since I've heard from you. No calls . . . no cards . . ."

"It was my understanding that you didn't want me to call you."

He was right, of course. The night she had given him back his ring she had told him not to call her again. She had wanted the break to be simple and uncomplicated. But her battered ego resented the fact that he'd been able to comply with her wishes so wholeheartedly.

She decided a change of subject was in order, so she reached for the Powder Puff folder. "I suppose you're wanting the preliminary information on the Powder Puff account?"

"Not this morning. If you can have it to me by midweek, that should be soon enough."

"Sure, no problem. I'll work on it tonight."

"It won't interfere with you and Dinkler?"

"Winkler," she corrected him, wishing he'd never seen the balloons.

"Sorry. Winkler. I don't want to interfere with your personal life. I understand you've been putting in a lot of hours lately."

"More than I care to," she admitted.

"Well, we'll see if we can change that." He smiled, settling back in his chair comfortably. "No use letting work interfere with our personal lives."

"No, we can't do that." Carly smiled back.

"Although Mireille never complains," he added.

Carly's smile tightened. *Mireille?*

Apparently in no hurry to leave, he smiled at her. "You do much dancing anymore?"

"All the time."

Carly! her conscience screamed. How could she mislead him that way? She hadn't gone dancing in a year. And who was Mireille?

"You still good?"

"Oh, I don't know," she said modestly. "What about you? You and . . . Mireille . . . it was Mireille?"

"Yeah, Mireille."

Her heart sank. So he had found someone else. "Interesting name—is it English?"

"French."

"Yes—" It would be. "Does Mireille enjoy dancing?"

He shrugged. "Not really."

"Oh, I'm sorry." Hee-hee-hee-hee. "I know you've always enjoyed it so much."

"Yeah," He shrugged again. "Mireille thinks that she's all feet."

They laughed.

"Guess that's the breaks." Dex stood up, extending a hand of friendship to her. "I'm looking forward to our working together again."

"Same here." Carly took his hand, ignoring the way his touch set off the swarm of butterflies in her stomach.

"Friends?" he asked.

"Friends."

They shook on it.

He walked to the door, then paused and turned around. "By the way, buddy, would you mind if I took the card for that balloon place? I want to order one of those balloon bouquets for Mireille. I think she might get a kick out of it."

"No . . . be happy to."

"Thanks." He winked.

Carly forced her smile to remain agreeable. "Of course."

"Thanks, kiddo. You always were a good sport."

She smiled lamely. "You're welcome."

He turned away, and a moment later she could hear him whistling as he walked down the hallway.

Stalking over to the door, she heaved it shut,

bringing Janis, who was sitting behind the reception desk, nearly off her seat.

Good sport, my foot, she thought.

Mireille, she seethed.

The door opened again, and Carly glanced up to find Dex peering around the corner questioningly.

"Did you say something?"

She shook her head mutely.

"Oh . . . sorry."

The door closed, and Carly stared at the balloons. She was going to throw them out.

"A what?"

Carly stared back at Martin Friday morning, dumbfounded.

"A softball game! Doesn't that sound great?"

Actually, it didn't. If Martin wanted Carly's honest opinion, an interoffice softball game sounded more in the realm of a nightmare.

"Company picnic's coming up," Martin reminded her. "And I said to myself while I was in the shower this morning, 'Martin, old boy, what are you going to do for entertainment this year?' And suddenly, while I was soaped to the eyeballs, the answer came to me. A softball game! Between marketing and R&D!"

"Between *departments*?" Carly asked incredulously. The two departments had enough trouble coexisting without a competitive ball game to aggravate the situation.

"Of course! Nothing builds team spirit better than a good old friendly ball game," Martin enthused.

Carly's heart sank. It was clear that he had fallen in love with the idea. "Martin—speaking of marketing, I've been meaning to talk to you about Dex—"

"Oh, I know. You're upset because I didn't tell you he was rejoining the firm."

"I think you should have mentioned—"

"You were away, and Dex didn't want me to," Martin said. "But don't look so worried. Dex assures me that you and he are still friends, and believe me, you'll enjoy the softball game once you've gotten your team together," Martin promised.

"*My* team?" Carly said lamely.

"Certainly—oh—you're captain of R&D's team," Martin said as if it were something she should have known all along. "And Dex has agreed to captain the marketing team."

Carly rose slowly to her feet. "Now, wait a minute, Martin." It was one thing to have to get a team together, but entirely another to have to compete against Dex. She *couldn't* compete against Dex. He did everything so effortlessly, while she was naturally uncoordinated. She was going to come out of this looking like a fool!

Martin completely misread her concern. "Oh, if you're worried about Dex, I've already checked with him. He says he doesn't have a problem with it if you don't."

Carly's brows arched resentfully. "Oh, really?"

"Not at all." Martin smiled, shaking his head. "That Dex. There's a real sport."

"Yeah, a real sport. Martin, I don't know anything about softball!" Carly protested. "Can't you get David to captain the team?"

"No, David's going to be on vacation."

"What about Ben?"

"Already tried. He can't—he has fallen arches."

She tried one more time. "Jeff?"

Martin shrugged apologetically. "Detests the game."

"So do I!" And she had a feeling that she was going to hate it even more by the time this conversation was over.

Which she did, vehemently, by the time Martin left her office whistling a few minutes later.

Captain of a softball team!

Snorting with disgust, she snatched up her coffee cup. On top of everything else she had to do, she was now captain of a softball team.

A softball team!

Restless, she strode down the hallway toward the coffee machine. Her mind turned on her, filling her with visions of a Smores and cups of rich, creamy hot chocolate. . . .

No. She had to think of something besides her growling stomach. It had been years since she'd played ball. Lord! She wasn't sure she even owned a mitt anymore. What she remembered about softball could be tattooed on a gnat's behind.

She'd been second-string catcher in junior high and spent most of her time on the bench.

Dex, on the other hand, she recalled, had played on a college team.

Well, wasn't this going to be *special*!

By late afternoon word about the ball game had spread. When they saw her coming down the hall, members of Carly's department scattered like rats deserting a sinking ship.

"Run, you cowards," she'd shouted behind their spineless, retreating backs. "But your names are on the list anyway!"

Dieting was hell.

Before the day was over, at least five people from marketing had stopped by her office to ask if playing against Dex was going to be a problem.

After the fifth denial, Carly went into her office, slammed the door, and screamed. When she'd finished, she drew a deep breath and smiled, feeling much better.

Then her gaze had fallen on the calendar. She'd groaned. Damn! She had promised to have dinner with Hayden tonight.

Reaching for the phone, she dialed Hayden's office.

"Hi," she said when his secretary put her through to him.

"Hi, there. How does Chinese sound for dinner this evening?"

"I'm sorry, Hayden, but I'm buried in work," she confessed. "Would you be too disappointed if I canceled again?" She realized that this was the third time in as many weeks that she'd begged off, but with her diet she couldn't eat anything anyway.

"No—but I would be happy to pick up some takeout and drop by the office later."

"That's sweet, but I'm on another diet," she confessed.

"*Another* one?"

Carly stiffened resentfully. Men just did not understand a woman's plight. "I'm really serious about this one."

Hayden was, as always, all politeness. "I could bring salads," he offered.

"That's so nice of you, but I think I'll just work for a while, then go home and soak in a hot tub." Something about dieting wore her out.

"Perhaps tomorrow night, then?"

"We'll see."

"By the way, I gave your name to a client I spoke with today. He's head of a new company, and they have an amazing product. I told him you'd be just the person to help him get that little gadget to the right people. His name is—" Carly could hear Hayden rustling through his pile of notes—"let's see . . . yes, Howard Anderson. He should be contacting you soon—and if he doesn't, let me know. Howard could be a fairly sizable account."

Carly closed her eyes wearily. Why did Hayden insist on giving her name to everyone he met? She was in R&D—not sales. And even if she weren't, didn't he think she could get her own clients?

Dex had never interfered in her work. In fact, just the opposite. He'd always been a staunch stand-on-your-own-two-feet kind of guy. "Get out there and rustle those bushes for yourself," he'd say, and she could remember a time when she had resented his saying that to her.

But he'd been right. Whenever she had a victory, she was proud. And she had to admit, she derived more satisfaction in the project. She'd grown up during the past year, both personally and professionally, and a measure of that was due to Dex and the values that he had drilled into her stubborn head.

"Thank you, Hayden. That was very nice of you."

"You're welcome . . . may I call you this evening?"

"If you like."

"Don't forget, the potential client's name is—"

"Howard Anderson."

"Right."

She hung up, wishing Hayden would stick to being an attorney.

Later that evening Carly trailed through her bedroom, spooning soup from a bowl into her mouth. She'd gotten home after nine. Again.

Disappearing into the bathroom, she ran a tub scented with her favorite bubble bath.

She let her robe drop to the floor and sank into the steamy water, her eyes closing in satisfaction.

Outside, the patter of rain fell softly on the rooftop as she sighed, slipping deeper into the aromatic water.

Her eyes suddenly popped open as Dex, uninvited, entered her mind.

It was the rain . . . memories of rainy nights and long, passionate Sunday afternoons making love . . .

She groaned. How could she work with him and not remember? How could she see him each day, then return to an empty apartment each night?

What's the difference? She argued with herself. She'd come home to an empty apartment every night for a year.

But there *was* a difference. Though Carly had insisted they maintain separate apartments while they were engaged, Dex had spent most of his time at hers.

And now that he was back Carly knew she was going to be in for some long, lonely, soul-searching nights.

She reminded herself that it was her choice to give him up.

Holding her nose, Carly slid beneath the water to block out the chafing voice. She didn't need to be reminded that she had made a mistake. If the past year without Dex hadn't driven home the point, the unexpected sight of him walking into the meeting Monday morning had.

The phone rang as she was toweling off an hour later.

Glancing at the clock, she was surprised to see

that it was almost ten. Hayden. She knotted the sash on her robe and hurried to answer it.

"Hello?"

"Carly?"

Carly sank down onto the side of the bed weakly. "Yes?"

"Sorry to call so late—I hope I didn't disturb you?" Dex sat in his office with the preliminary reports on the Powder Puff account spread out before him.

"No, in fact, I just got out of the tub."

He leaned back, recalling the way she looked after a bath. Her hair would be curled from the damp heat of the long soak, her skin pink and fragrant from the hot water into which she invariably poured a generous amount of bath oil. Gardenias. He shifted in the chair, annoyed to feel the first signs of arousal.

"Where are you?" she asked.

"At the office."

"Still?"

"I've never seen so much damn work," he admitted.

"I know." Carly had struggled with the Powder Puff account for over six weeks, making little headway.

"I wanted to clarify a point or two on the research." Dex was surprised to find that he was having difficulty concentrating. Just a few minutes before he'd considered his questions too important to wait until morning. Now he realized he could have waited . . . yet he had felt compelled to hear her voice again.

"Okay, shoot."

He fired several questions at her which to her relief she was able to answer efficiently—and with an impressive amount of knowledge if she did say so herself.

When she finished her explanations, she could have sworn she heard a new respect in his voice. "Well, I'm impressed, Winters. You've done a damn good job."

"Thank you." Why it should mean more coming from him than from anyone else, Carly wasn't sure, but it did.

"Well, that ought to do it." Dex paused and Carly wondered if he was searching for an excuse to extend the conversation. "Hope I didn't bother you," he said.

"Not at all."

He chuckled as if she had said something funny.

Taken aback, she asked quickly, "Did I say something amusing?"

"No, I just seem to be having a hard time convincing myself that you have a personal life of your own now." He paused again, apparently waiting for her to convince him.

Carly could hear rain pattering on the windowsills. An ache began to build in her—one she identified with Dex. The ache grew more restrictive when she thought about the way they used to lie in each other's arms, exchanging husky whispers . . . stolen kisses . . . touching . . . tasting. . . . She had missed that. No. She'd missed him.

At the moment her heart felt more empty than her stomach. She might have been intimidated by Dex at the office, but after hours they had been perfect equals. And now he was back with a new love in his life, while she had her prized independence.

Funny, how being on her own could feel so lonely.

"Well, it seems you have a private life of your own," she said coolly, knowing that she shouldn't be opening the subject for debate. "By the way, how's Mireille?"

"She's great."

"Been dating long?"

"We don't actually date. We just sort of hang out together."

"Oh, now nice."

"Yeah, she's okay."

"Have you known her long?"

"About a year."

A year. A year! He certainly hadn't pined over her very long.

"Did she enjoy the balloons?" she asked, hoping to betray none of her hurt in her voice.

"You know, she didn't say, and I've been so busy I haven't thought to ask."

"Oh."

"How about you? You and this Hayden serious?"

"Oh . . . Hayden's very nice."

"Yeah, so I've heard. A lawyer?"

Dex wondered why he'd even brought up the subject. This wasn't the plan. The plan was to come back to Chicago and pick up the pieces of his life. The past year had been miserable, but, mercifully, the initial hurt had passed, replaced by resigned acceptance, then a renewed determination. It had taken him months to work though his seesawing emotions, but he'd finally decided that he was going to make her want to marry him again. But he wasn't about to grovel. He'd give her enough time to come back to him on her own terms.

He'd known that they'd been arguing more than usual before their breakup, but he'd never considered their disagreements serious. They both were competitive people, and he'd found it increasingly hard to get along with her. But he'd believed that their differences had been confined to the office, didn't really affect their personal life. When she'd walked in one day and handed him back his ring with the excuse that she hadn't felt sure whether she wanted the marriage, he'd been so bowled over, he hadn't even replied.

Now, if he had it to do over, he wouldn't have taken it as calmly.

"Yes—Hayden's a lawyer. What about it!" Hunger pangs made Carly's response sharper than she intended.

"Are you dieting again?"

"What makes you say that?" she challenged him.

"I don't know—you just sound like you're dieting again."

"Well, I'm not." Her heart sank. He had noticed her Petunia Pig thighs.

Hang up, Dex. She's in one of her witchy moods. Yet he heard himself saying, "What do you think about the softball game?"

"I think it's stupid."

He chuckled. "I'll take it easy on you."

"Don't bother. I'm quite capable of holding my own against you."

His voice softened. "Yeah, I haven't forgotten."

She wished he wasn't being so nice. He should just say what she was sure he'd been dying to say to her for the past year—that she'd won the turkey-of-the-decade award and that he'd made it just fine without Carly Winters in his life.

"Carly."

She tensed, having a feeling that the conversation was about to take a personal turn.

"Yes?"

"One question, then I promise I'll never bring the subject up again."

She sighed, knowing the answer before he even asked. Hadn't the question lay like an anchor in her heart for over a year now?

"Is it necessary for you to ask it?" She had hoped he would just let bygones be bygones.

Play it cool, Dex, nice and easy. "I'll admit that at first I thought it wasn't. I figured that if you wanted to break the engagement, I wasn't about to stop you. But when I walked into the board-room the other morning and saw you sitting there, it occurred to me that maybe I should have asked what the hell I'd done."

Drawing a deep breath, Carly sighed. "It wasn't you—it was me."

"Could you narrow that down some?"

"It's hard, Dex."

Dex shifted in his chair. He knew it would be hard. He didn't need to have that pointed out to him.

He tried to help. "Do you feel I pushed you too hard?"

"No."

"No?"

"No . . . I always felt that I was . . . competing with you."

"Did I make you feel that way?" he asked quietly.

"No, I just felt that way. . . . I was beginning to feel suffocated and stupid and inadequate."

"I made you feel that way?"

"No, not you—me! That's why I broke the engagement. . . . I just didn't want to have to compete with the man I married." She supposed that's why she continued to date Hayden when she knew the relationship was headed nowhere. She wasn't in love with Hayden, and never would be. But there wasn't a thing about Hayden to threaten her.

"I find that hard to believe, tig—"

"Don't call me that." The affectionate term brought back too many memories.

"Okay," he conceded, "but you're not going to be happy with any man who doesn't challenge you."

"How do you know?" She had already begun to suspect it, but she wondered how he could know for certain.

He laughed, causing her knees to turn to molasses. "Let's just say that I do."

"Let's just say good night," she suggested. It was obvious that he wasn't sorry they broke up, just curious. He had replaced her so fast that it made her head swim!

"Okay. Good night."

"Good night."

Slamming the receiver back into place, she made a beeline for the refrigerator.

Drizzling chocolate sauce over the rest of a Munching Good double fudge cherry cheesecake with almonds, she assured herself that this was only a temporary setback.

She wasn't still in love with Dex.

She wasn't.

Three

Carly's mind was made up. She would be the best research director Dex had ever had the pleasure of working with. She no longer felt obligated to compete with him; she just wanted to do her job and let him do his. They would be a professional business team.

Whatever they had once shared, was over. *Finito.* And she wasn't going to give it another thought.

Her resolve wobbled only slightly when she walked into his office later that morning and saw him sitting behind the desk looking too handsome for words. If this diet didn't kill her, Dex was going to give her a gastric ulcer.

Naturally, the dark blue silk tie he was wearing was in impeccable good taste, not to mention the tweed blazer and navy blue slacks. The man had class, no doubt about it. Good looks, talent, and class. Way to go, Carly. You know how to get rid of 'em, babe, she told herself.

It was just this sort of depressing setback that made the glass of Weight BeGone ball up in her stomach like a wad of cement.

"Morning," she murmured quietly.

Dex glanced up, and his smile nearly unraveled her. "Morning."

Drawing a deep breath, she marched to the nearest chair and sat down.

Finito. She repeated the word like a mantra.

"Cruller?" Dex absently picked up a box of doughnuts and extended to her.

"No, thanks."

He glanced up from the printout he was studying. "You sick?"

"No." She shrugged with a forced smile. Lord, she hoped saliva wasn't drooling out of the corners of her mouth. "Just not hungry." At least he hadn't mentioned the D word.

Opening her folder, her hands trembled as she tried to locate the Powder Puff questionnaire. Desperately, she tried to ignore the smell of two crullers and the sweet roll coated with powdered sugar and loaded with raspberry jam that Dex was stuffing into his mouth.

At least it smelled like raspberry jam to Carly's aching taste buds.

He stirred cream—real cream—into his coffee, then stuck the stick into the corner of his mouth as he began to read from his own fact sheets.

He glanced up. "Coffee?"

"Thank you." She got up, poured herself a cup, and sat down again.

To her surprise, the meeting went well. She didn't feel threatened or resentful, as she'd thought she would. And Dex showed no signs of discomfort, though she admitted he seemed preoccupied. Preoccupied with eating! Those damn doughnuts.

At one point she was forced to walk around the desk and lean near him to run over some old research results. If the smell of fresh pastry—light and mouth-watering, baked just that morning, oozing with a zillion-calories-a-spoonful jams and icings and powdered sugar—didn't have her nerves running ragged, the aroma of his aftershave completed her agony.

The elegant scent reminded her that she'd purchased a bottle of the same fragrance for Hayden at Christmas.

Unfortunately, Hayden's body chemistry had reduced the sophisticated scent of the cologne to a smell similar to rotting leaves.

She wasn't sure what was going to drive her over the edge first: the glass of Weight BeGone gyrating in her stomach, the sweet roll coated with powdered sugar and loaded with raspberry jam, or Dex.

Dex, she decided. The man did crazy things to her libido.

By the time the meeting was over, Carly's

nerves were strung as tight as a whipcord. The *finito* mantra just wasn't working.

For instance, she'd caught herself checking his neck for signs of Mireille twice—hickeys or something equally as disgusting—but he'd come up clean.

She knew she was being an idiot. She hoped he couldn't read minds.

Yet it was hard for her to think of anything but Dex, especially when he was making an effort to treat her so nice—so appallingly equal.

At times she almost wished that he'd revert to the old Dex and disagree with her once in a while. But he hadn't. Instead, he had painstakingly pointed out areas in her research plan that could be strengthened, at the same time discreetly sidestepping any issue that would endanger her ego.

As always, his suggestions were relevant—ones she wondered why she hadn't thought of herself. She could admit that he was good. Too good. She tried to ward away thoughts of just *how* good he was—*extremely* gifted, actually, in the bedroom, the living room, the shower, on the sofa—on rainy nights, during old movies . . .

She remembered the man had a knack for knowing just where and how and what to touch . . .

Dex asking her to repeat a set of figures brought her back to the present. She rummaged through her folder, confused.

"You sure you don't want a doughnut?" he asked absently.

"No, I don't want a doughnut!"

An hour later, the meeting finally concluded. "Well, that should do it." Dex leaned forward and helped himself to another sweet roll. "You'd better have one. It'll put you in a better mood."

"No, thanks." She sighed, eyeing the pastry wistfully. The Weight BeGone was leaving her like a fast freight on its way out of town. "I'll have these typed up and back on your desk by late afternoon." She stood up. "Anything else?"

"I think that covers it."

She started to leave when he said, "Winters, you've got a nice framework, kiddo."

Carly turned, hating the way she was tempted to flirt with him. "I assume you mean the project?"

He grinned, a slow and totally masculine assault that devoured her senses. "The project's okay too."

She smiled. "You really think so?"

"That you have a good framework or"—he wiggled his brows provocatively—"that you have a *nice* framework?"

"Seriously, Boomer. I really have gotten better, haven't I?"

He smiled. She didn't realize that she'd called him Boomer.

She frowned. "What's wrong?"

"Nothing."

He could see that she was taking her work seriously now, and he was encouraged. She had come a long way this past year and was getting better every day. Crossing his arms behind his head, he leaned back in his chair, taking a few moments to collect his thoughts. She was wearing red today, his favorite color on her.

Carly felt her cheeks growing warm under his lazy perusal. She prayed that he didn't notice the results of last night's cheesecake massacre.

"You're good, Carly. Why didn't Martin promote you into marketing? You're more than capable of handling the job."

Relief filled her. And elation. Dex wouldn't tell her she was good if she wasn't. That wasn't his style.

"Martin and I talked about it, but I didn't feel that I wanted marketing yet. Give me another year or two . . . then I'll be good enough to give you a run for your money, mister."

They smiled at each other, a nice, warm, okay-so-we-can-be-friends smile.

"Dream on, sweetheart."

Reverting to her John Wayne voice, Carly hitched her thumbs through her belt, reared back, and looked him straight in the eye. "Wahll now, don't you be so durn shore about that, pilgrim."

Dex sprang to his feet, his eyes narrowing into silly viperous slits. "Now, you just hold on thar. No person of the female persuasion speaks to Dex 'Clint-Eastwood-ain't-got-nothin'-on-me' Matthews that way! Slap leather, you wily sidewinder!"

They both whipped out imaginary pistols and fired at each other as the door to the office opened, and John Waterman, head of Powder Puff, entered.

Caught in the cross fire, John stood speechless, watching the exchange.

Carly glanced up and, upon seeing John, immediately ceased firing.

"Mr. Waterman?" she squeaked.

John "never-crack-a-smile" Waterman peered pretentiously back at her through a vapor of heavy imaginary gunpowder. "Ms. Winters," he returned stiffly.

Stepping around the desk, Dex casually extended his hand to one of Montrose's largest accounts. "John. Nice to see you."

Carly meekly gathered folders as Dex charmingly engaged John in a conversation involving his golf game.

A moment later she slipped out of Dex's office with the last sugar-coated roll packed with decadent raspberry jam, wrapped in a napkin.

Dex had tucked it into her hand on her way out.

That afternoon Carly decided to get down to serious business about the ball team. She knew now that she could work with Dex, but she wasn't sure how she was going to handle sharing her personal time with him.

Joanne, one of the newer researchers, offered to help organize the team, and Carly gladly accepted. She needed all the help she could get.

She didn't know diddly about softball, but she was good at organization. That was a start.

On her lunch hour she stopped in a bookstore and bought a book on softball. She planned to study it tonight, and that way she wouldn't appear quite so ignorant. There wasn't a doubt in her mind about the outcome of the game. It would be mass slaughter—her team lying on the field, beaten, embarrassed, shamed, defeated . . . their noses rubbed in the dirt. But R&D wasn't about to hand marketing a meaningless victory without a fight.

Carly would see to that.

"Hey, tig. How's the ol' team shaping up?"

"Fine, Boomer. And yours?"

"No sweat."

Carly passed Dex at the water fountain and kept going.

No sweat, she mimicked as she turned the corner and trucked on down the hallway.

Not surprising.

He had more jocks in his department than Imelda Marcos had sling-back pumps.

Dex walked past Carly on his way to the copy machine Thursday afternoon.

"Heard you're having trouble finding a pitcher," he called over his shoulder.

"Don't you wish."

"You're not?"

"Do you think I'd tell you if I were?"

"Maybe if you'd beg a little, I'd send you some of my rejects."

"Maybe you're suffering from a high fever and should go home and sleep it off."

Carly could hear him still chuckling as he disappeared down the hallway.

As Carly pulled into the parking lot Monday morning, she saw that Dex's car was already there.

His candy-apple-red Corvette with the license plate IAM#1 was taking up two parking places.

She found the office complex nearly empty when she entered. She smiled at the janitor as her footsteps echoed down the hallway.

" 'Morning, Frank."

" 'Morning, Ms. Winters."

"How's Edith today?"

Frank paused, leaning on his broom. "Doing real fine. She sure did appreciate the flowers you sent."

"I'm glad she enjoyed them. Tell her to take it easy and not overdo. I hear gallbladder surgery can take a while to get over."

"I'll tell her—and she said she wanted to have you over to dinner once she's up and around again."

"Make it porkchops!" Carly waved over her

shoulder as she stepped into the elevator and punched the button for the third floor. *Fried, with mashed potatoes and gravy.*

Dex was at his desk, preoccupied with some printouts when she entered his office. His eyes scanned the long columns as his pencil tapped a rhythmic beat against a pad of paper. Muzak played in the background, and Carly suddenly had the insane impulse to ask him to dance.

He glanced up when she breezed in.

"Hi."

"Hi."

He nodded toward the coffeepot. "Coffee's ready."

"You made coffee?"

"I am truly amazing."

"You truly are."

Well, some things change, she thought. There was a time when he would have insisted that *she* make the coffee. She hoped his conscientiousness was not due to Mireille's influence.

Removing her list of ongoing projects from a folder, she seated herself. A moment later Dex handed her a cup of the freshly brewed coffee.

She took a sip, wrinkling her nose. "Ye gads."

"Don't knock it."

She was relieved to see that instead of the customary doughnuts and sweet rolls, wedges of fresh melon and juicy ripe strawberries dominated the platter this morning.

He offered the tray to her. "Fruit?"

She helped herself to a slice of cantaloupe, then, reconsidering, took another.

After all, a dieter was allowed fruit.

The meeting began. Dex asked for an overview of each client: company, background, product, and what preliminary work had been done. While Carly ticked off the status of each account, he took notes in a bold scrawl on a legal pad.

"Any accounts on inactive?"

"Several. In both research and marketing."

"I understand Arnie Whittaker wasn't interested in 'romancing' clients or keeping in touch with former accounts?"

"Not in the least. As long as they came to us, Arnie was happy. We've had several accounts as lucrative as Powder Puff in the past year, but because of poor management I'm afraid Arnie lost most of them."

"Then I guess I should begin getting in touch with the inactives, reintroduce myself to the ones I know, and see what we can do to stir up some business. Then we'll see about getting you and your staff some help."

"Oh, Dex, could you?" The past few weeks had been a nightmare. Overworked and understaffed.

"Consider it done."

The morning sun was shining through the slats of the blinds, catching the light in her hair. A cute, blue-eyed blonde. That's what Dex had always considered her. She wasn't beautiful or glamorous, but he didn't want that type of woman. He'd always found her girl-next-door quality irresistible.

Pain shot through him. An ache, starting somewhere between his rib cage and the cavity of his chest, refused to ease up. Lord, he missed her.

Times like this made him wonder if he hadn't made a mistake by coming back. He'd thought that he could work with her again. But sitting here with her like this, listening to her friendly chatter, he realized that he just plain missed her. He missed her cuddled next to him on a rainy night, sharing a bowl of popcorn and watching old Tracy and Hepburn movies.

They had seen *The African Queen* so many times they each knew the dialogue by heart. He missed making love to her; he missed holding her hand; he missed laughing at a joke or a funny incident they'd shared at the office that day.

Her words rang hollowly in his head. *I felt incompetent, stupid, and inadequate, Dex.*

He'd never realized he'd made her feel that way.

Carly detected a subtle softening as he quietly closed his folder. Leaning back against his chair, he looked at her. "You look nice today."

"Thank you." She lowered her head. "I guess you've noticed I've gained a little weight?"

That's it, point it out to him, Carly, as if he couldn't see your Miss Piggy hips as it is.

"No," he said. "I hadn't noticed."

She lifted her gaze to meet his expression of amusement. "You wouldn't tell me if you had," she said.

She knew he'd condemn bad work if she were guilty of it in a New York minute, but he had never criticized the extra pounds she was doomed to carry.

He grinned. "Of course not. Do you think I've lost my mind?"

"No, but I know how men are. If a woman gains a pound—"

"Well, I suppose that would depend on the man." Getting to his feet, he filled his cup again. "Personally, I've always liked you just the way you are."

"That's very nice, but I know you don't mean it."

She left the office a moment later, wondering if things like that weren't why she still loved him— he could say something as simple as "I like you the way you are" and convince her that he meant it.

Carly caught herself. You are not still in love with him, and even if you were—there's Mireille. There was no doubt that the little French woman—no doubt size four and not a smidge of cellulite on her—would never hand him back to Carly without a fight. And what made her think for one minute that he would even want to come back?

Men like Dex Matthews rarely give a woman a second chance to walk out on them again, she reminded herself.

Greta was combing her hair in front of the mirror when Carly entered the ladies' room.

Great. The line for Dex Matthews begins at the rear.

"I hear you and Dex have been spending a lot of time together. Anything serious developing?" Greta asked casually.

Greta was not known for possessing an over-abundance of tact.

Grabbing a paper towel, Carly busied herself with sopping up the puddles standing on the countertop so she could set her purse down.

There might be nothing left but friendship between her and Dex, but serving him up to Greta on a gold platter with a plump apple stuck in his mouth was something else again. Mireille would have to fend for herself.

"We work well together," she mumbled.

"Uh-huhhh." The blonde carefully outlined her generous lips with a bright red lip pencil.

"Have you signed up for the softball team?" Carly asked, hoping to switch her to another track.

"As a matter of fact, I haven't. Gee"—Greta reached for a tissue to blot her lips—"it's been years since I played."

Carly had to admit she was a bit surprised. Greta the Goddess? In a sweaty shirt? "You've played softball?"

She couldn't begin to imagine the tall blonde with legs that started at her ears, on a ball field. The thought of Greta's three-inch acrylic nails wedged into a softball mitt was actually painful.

"Sure. I pitched for our college team."

Pitched?

Bingo!

"You're kidding! Listen, we need a pitcher desperately. How about signing up for the game?"

Greta preened before the mirror, obviously a legend in her own mind. "Oh . . . I don't know . . . Dex is managing marketing's team?" Greta asked.

"Yeah."

"Gee . . . I don't know." Greta pivoted sideways to admire her reflection from another angle. "It could be fun . . . I suppose."

Carly knew exactly what kind of "fun" Greta had in mind. She'd had her eye on Dex from the day he'd arrived at Montrose, and she'd never been very subtle about her intentions.

But beggars couldn't be choosers. If the lady could get a ball within fifteen feet of home plate, she was in.

"Can I put your name down?"

"Oh . . ." Greta examined her profile a little longer. It seemed she couldn't bear to turn it loose. "I suppose."

"Great."

Two down, seven to go.

"Speaking of Dex, I guess you've heard?" Carly nonchalantly pulled out her own tube of lipstick and studied her lips in the mirror—lips that Dex had lost himself in in the heat of passion many, many times. Eat your heart out, Greta baby.

"Heard what?" Greta perked up with interest.

"About Dex."

Greta's brows rose. "What about Dex?"

"He's involved with someone."

Greta frowned. "With whom?"

Carly shrugged. "A French girl."

"French." It came out strangled.

Carly shrugged innocently. "That's what I hear."

So bug off, sweetie! Neither one of them had a chance.

"Are they serious?"

Dropping her tube of lipstick back into her purse, Carly smiled. "Oh, will you look at the time?" She grinned. "Late again."

Emerging from the bathroom a moment later, Carly felt giddy with power.

She didn't know why she should feel so good about being such a worm.

But she did.

In fact, the whole incident had made up for that one pitifully thin, 98-percent fat free, only twenty-five calories a slice ham smunched between two rice cakes that she'd eaten for lunch.

Or almost.

Four

With Greta's name firmly added to the roster, all Carly needed now were a couple of hot outfielders—preferably ringers, if she could find a couple she could bribe.

By noon Friday she had decided to settle for lukewarm outfielders.

By four she again lowered her goal. Breathing was now the only requirement to play on R&D's team. If a body could breathe, it would make her team.

"Well, you're not going to believe this."

At five Carly glanced up to see Janis standing in the doorway holding a large box.

"What is it?"

"Shirts."

Carly frowned. "What?"

"Another one of Martin's brainstorms." Janis

entered the office, carrying the box to Carly's desk. "Get a load of these babies."

Carly opened the box, lifted out a shirt, and held it to her. It didn't look large enough. She checked the label, then held it up to herself again. It was the smallest large she'd even seen. Oh, great, Martin had had the company logo silk-screened on the front, and the player's first name emblazoned across the back.

She pawed through the dozen shirts, hoping that some were bigger than others. A moment later she gave up. They were all the same size. And not one would work, certainly not with will-you-get-a-load-of-them-headlights Greta at home plate. The men would be slobbering all over their spikes.

"Let's try one on," Janis warned. "It isn't too late to reorder."

Carly wasn't sure why, but she was the one elected to try on the shirt. She slinked down the hall a minute later, trying to hide the shirt behind her back. Maybe she could tell Martin that the shirts had been lost. No, he could track that down too easy.

Stolen! That might be worth a try.

Removing her blouse, she dragged the T-shirt over her head. Turning back to the mirror, she groaned.

Montrose was spelled out in big black fuzzy letters across the front of the shirt—which was okay for the men, but it spelled big trouble for the women.

The first big black O caught the tip of one nipple, while the second O circled the other.

Exquisite. Simply exquisite.

Turning, Carly studied her profile in the mirror, trying to picture what Greta's chest would do to the big black Os.

Carly cracked open the bathroom door and peered outside. The coast was clear.

Darting out, Carly double-timed down the hall, making a beeline for her office. Sprinting inside, she slammed the door, then leaned her forehead against it to draw a deep breath.

Safe.

Jamming her hands to her hips, she thrust her chest out dramatically and turned around, grinning cheekily. "What do you think?"

The silence that met her was deafening.

Dex and two gray-haired gentlemen stared at the front of her shirt, looking impressed.

She felt her face turn the color of catsup.

"Well"—Dex cleared his voice—"personally, I think it's great, don't you, Frank?"

Frank wasn't saying, but his eyes were about to bug out of his sockets.

"Er . . . yes . . . yes . . . quite nice," the second gentleman supplied hesitantly. Then the old rake snickered. "I wouldn't object to playin' against 'em!"

"Janis?" Carly's eyes went to Dex wildly. "What happened to Janis?"

For the first time since she'd known him, Dex

looked a little tense. "She mentioned something about phones ringing?"

If the floor had opened up and swallowed her, Carly would have been forever grateful.

As usual, Dex calmly stepped in to save the day. "Gentlemen, I'd like you to meet a very special lady, Carly Winters."

Relief flooded the two older men's faces as they reached out to shake Carly's hand. "Ms. Winters," they murmured.

Carly could see the two men read more into Dex's introduction than was there, but she wasn't about to correct the misunderstanding.

"The shirts are great." Dex squeezed her shoulder. "Marketing has challenged R&D to a softball game at the company picnic in a couple of weeks," he explained. "Carly's been going from office to office, modeling the shirts in an effort to boost team spirit."

"Oh . . . that's nice." The two men nodded agreeably, but Carly could see they didn't have the faintest idea of what was going on.

"Carly, Frank Wilcox and Rand Silverton. Frank and Rand are the new owners of Peek-A-Boo Nursery Products."

Carly finally managed to find her voice. Recovering, she extended her hand and smiled. "Frank, Rand. So nice to meet you."

Shaking each man's hand, Carly heard herself babbling something that she hoped didn't sound as stupid as she felt.

"Carly will be in charge of your account," Dex

told the two men. He paused, his gaze going back to Carly's. "I think you'll find her to be an exceptional young woman."

Frank's and Rand's eyes traveled innocently back to the big black Os on Carly's T-shirt.

"Yes," Frank murmured, "we can see that."

"Absolutely," Rand added in a tone that said he really, really meant it.

Ball practice got under way. Even though Carly had studied the book on softball until her eyes were bloodshot, the first session was every bit as bad as she had expected. She didn't have a player who could catch a ball—nor one who even wanted to.

The men claimed that they were out of shape, though Carly noticed that their eyeballs were getting an aerobic workout ogling the women who'd shown up in shorts.

Thank heaven it rained Thursday morning. By noon the rain gauges had collected a quarter of an inch, and the pewter-gray skies showed no visible signs of clearing in time for ball practice that afternoon.

The coffee machine was surrounded by the usual slackers when Carly walked out of her office. She could see that they had all been praying for a monsoon.

Sticking her cup beneath the spigot, she said casually, "Guess what, guys? Martin has decided to cancel the game." She reached for a package of Sweet 'n' Low and sprinkled it into her coffee. "Guess there'll be no more after-work ball practices."

The group went bananas, whooping it up, slapping each other's backs, bumping bottoms, and exchanging high-fives.

Carly calmly dropped the stirrer into the wastebasket.

"Just kidding about Martin canceling the game," she said when the din finally subsided.

Faces fell like the Alamo.

"But, since it's raining, that means we'll have to practice twice on Saturday." Carly picked up her cup and started back toward her office. "You be sure to be on time."

Having a free afternoon was an unexpected but welcome bonus. Carly left work a few minutes early and headed straight for the courthouse. Her car license was due, and she'd misplaced her personal property receipt, which meant she had to get a new one. As she hopped across growing puddles in the parking lot, she mentally cursed herself for leaving her umbrella at home. By the time she'd reached her car, her feet were soaked.

Twenty minutes from the office, the car gave a funny lurch and the steering wheel jerked to one side. Her heart in her throat, Carly glanced into her rearview mirror as she eased her car to the side of the road and set the emergency brake.

Even before she looked, she knew what had

happened. A flat tire. The second one this month. Obviously, a puncture. The wheel was setting on the rim, so there was no hope of coaxing her car to a gas station without ruining the whole tire.

Giving up all thoughts of salvaging her hair or her suit, Carly hauled herself out of the car, unlocked the trunk, and peered inside dismally. The spare was flat. Correction. The *spare* was on the car and the original tire that had gone flat two weeks earlier was still flat. She'd meant to drop it off at a tire shop to have it repaired, but with everything else going on, she'd forgotten.

A box of Oreos would be comforting right about now. Double stuff, Oreo cookies.

Glancing at the bumper-to-bumper traffic, she weighed the prospect of hitching a ride, then abandoned the idea.

Being mugged and left for dead wouldn't necessarily improve her day.

She trudged off in the direction of a phone she'd passed about a mile back.

"Singing in the rain, just singing in the rain, what a glorioussssss—" She gasped as a semi blew by, drenching her with a wash of nasty road water.

Fifteen minutes later she spotted the phone near the off ramp. Pumping in a quarter, she dialed Hayden's number.

His secretary answered with crisp proficiency, "Winkler and Bartholomew Law Offices."

"Hi, Mary. Let me speak to Hayden."

"Hayden's in court right now—Carly?"

"Yeah"—Carly glanced at her watch—"have any idea what time he'll be out?"

"Late, I'm afraid. Do you need something?"

"Yeah, I've had another flat tire."

"Oh, dear. Do you want me to call a tow truck for you?"

Carly sighed, surveying the line of heavy traffic outside the phone booth. A tow truck would take hours. "No, I'll see if I can catch Janis before she leaves the office."

She hung up and dug inside her purse again. Great. Only one more quarter. She had to make it count.

She dialed the office, praying that Janis would still be there. Glancing at her watch, she saw that it was two minutes after five.

Her heart lifted then fell when Janis's voice came over the wire via the answering machine. "Good evening. Montrose Research is closed for the day. If you'd like to leave—"

Carly clipped the receiver back into place.

She thought of Martin's private line. He often worked late.

She dialed the operator and asked her to place a collect call to Martin Montrose at his executive suite.

Martin picked up the phone on the second ring.

"Will you accept a collect call from Carly Winters?" the operator asked crisply.

"Put her through," he replied.

"Martin?" Carly sagged with relief. "Am I ever glad you're there."

"Carly? What's going on?"

"I've had a flat on the expressway."

"Do you have a spare?"

"Well . . . yes and no." She hated to let him know that she was such an airhead, but he probably already suspected it. "I have a spare, but it's flat too. I hate to ask, Martin . . . but I need help . . . "

"Of course, let me make a quick call, then I'm on my way."

Carly gave Martin exact directions to where she was stranded, then hung up and huddled deeper into the lining of her jacket.

It was going to be a long night.

"Hold the door!"

Dex automatically reached out to block the elevator doors from closing as Martin came hurrying down the hall.

Still struggling into his raincoat, Martin stepped inside the car. "Thanks."

The doors closed, and the elevator began its humming descent.

"Working late again?"

"No," Martin glanced at his watch anxiously. "Gloria's made reservations at the Henessey Inn for seven, but I'm afraid a problem has come up. Carly called, and she's had a flat on the expressway. I called the restaurant and left word that I would be late, but Gloria will be there any minute. . . . She must've already left the house; I couldn't reach her there." Martin shrugged. "It's our anniversary . . . ."

Dex shook his head mutely. Carly had never been good with details. "Let me guess. Carly's spare is flat?"

Martin glanced at him knowingly. "Yes."

Dex nodded.

The elevator reached the first floor. The door slid open, and Dex and Martin exited, matching long-legged strides as they crossed the lobby.

"Look, there's no sense in you keeping Gloria waiting," Dex said. "I'll go after Carly, and you go on to the restaurant—"

Martin accepted the offer before it was out of Dex's mouth. "Do you mind?"

"No, I was just going to grab a hamburger on the way home, then work on the Jekin's Chicken account."

"Matthews, I owe you one." Martin slapped Dex on the back gratefully. "Sure you don't mind?"

"I don't mind."

Martin told Dex where Carly was stranded, and the two men agreed that she wouldn't be hard to find.

Twenty minutes later Dex spotted Carly's blue Camaro sitting on the side of the busy expressway. The windshield wipers flapped noisily to keep up with the steady downpour as he pulled his Corvette behind her Camaro and stopped.

Approaching her car, he grinned when he caught Carly slumped against the center console, sound asleep.

Tapping on the window, he managed to rouse her.

Carly opened her eyes to find Dex making a face at her through the window.

Scrambling to sit up, she rolled down the window. "What are you doing here?"

"At the moment? Backstroking. Let me in."

She flipped the lock on the door, then scooted over as he got in.

Two in one bucket seat was crowded but interesting. And nice. Carly considered climbing over the console to the passenger seat, but not for long. It felt too good to be this close to him again.

"Trouble, Winters?"

"Ain't it the way of life, Matthews?"

"Have you ever considered having your spare fixed?"

"Once—but I never followed through with it."

Breathe, Carly, she told herself. One breath at a time. He wasn't the best-looking man on earth. His aftershave didn't drive her wild. But if he didn't stop looking at her that way, she really wasn't going to be able to resist the urge to kiss him—or, worse, strip his clothes off like a hussy inside this cozy car with rain pattering down on the roof.

"Are you?"

Carly started as the sound of his voice penetrated her lusty thoughts. "No," she replied automatically.

Dex drew back defensively. "Hey, okay, just asking."

She wondered what he had just asked her that required a practical answer.

"What?" he asked, reacting to the confusion he saw in her eyes.

"What did you say?"

"I asked if you wanted me to get the spare fixed for you."

"Oh . . . well, no. I couldn't ask you to do that."

"Believe me, it would be less trouble than having to rescue you in a blinding rainstorm."

"I thought Martin was coming."

"Today is Martin and Gloria's anniversary. They had dinner plans."

"Oh, well, that's nice."

"I'll make you a deal. You hold the umbrella while I get the wheel off, then we'll take both tires to the gas station and wait until they're finished."

For someone down to only three operating tires, Carly figured she didn't have much choice. "Okay, but . . . skip the umbrella. I forgot to bring one."

"I would have bet on it."

Carly rummaged through her purse to come up with a compact. Able to see by the passing car lights, she frowned. "Jeez!"

Stepping out of the car, Dex stripped out of his tie and jacket and handed them to her. She pitched them onto the seat, then got out to help.

She sorted through the tools in her trunk, located the metric wrench, and handed it to him. It was pouring buckets as Dex jacked up the car, then squatted beside the wheel, removed the hubcap, and began loosening lug bolts.

"You might as well get into my car," he called above the din of semis passing in an endless stream. He could see that she was already drenched to the core.

"No, I want to help!"

Removing the wheel, Dex rolled the tire back to the Corvette, opened the back, and set it inside.

He walked back to the Camaro, removed the original flat tire from the trunk, and rolled it back to the Corvette, motioning for Carly to follow.

"Get in!"

"My clothes are wet, I'll ruin the leather seat," she protested.

"Get into the car, Carly!"

She meekly opened the door and slid inside the Corvette.

Déjà-vu besieged her as she surveyed the interior of the familiar car. The rich smell of leather, cherry, and Gianfranco Ferré surrounded her. Running her fingers along the console, she recalled the way Dex used to pull her onto his lap to neck while they waited at stoplights.

She found her arms suddenly covered in goose bumps as she lay her head back, trying to force the painful memories aside, but the knot in her throat was the size of a golf ball and refused to yield.

What should she do now? Should she just swallow her pride and tell him that she was sorry? That she'd made a mistake when she broke the engagement? Should she simply admit that she was more in love with him now than she'd ever been in her entire life. . . .

Would it do any good to confess to him that the past year had been nothing short of hell, and that the times he had picked up the phone and found no one there, it had been her on the other end, just wanting to hear the sound of his voice?

Maybe if she asked—no, begged him to take her back, he would. Maybe he would understand if she explained that she really never once doubted her love for him . . . only her ability to retain her own identity once they were married?

Yes, she could say all those things and Dex, being Dex, would be generous and understanding and would say that he, too, was sorry that she'd only now realized her error, but he would explain that the truth of the matter was that it was simply too late: he had found someone else.

Then he would suggest in his nice, crisp, let's-cut-the-crap-and-get-to-the-point way that she should do the same.

Adios, Ms. "Go-and-find-your-own-identity-if-it's-so-damn-important-to-you" Winters.

See if he cared.

Funny how her identity had seemed so important to her at one time. Now she could be happy just being a part of him.

The door opened, and Dex slid onto the driver's seat. There wasn't a dry thread on him. "Judas Priest! It's a monsoon out there!"

Carly grinned. It was all she could do to keep from crawling over the console, wrapping her arms around his neck, and kissing him senseless, something she'd done so many times in the past that it would come as natural to her as eating.

Instead, she attempted to say something blasé, witty, and sexy that came out sounding mundane. "It's a mess, isn't it?"

A little later Dex pulled into a service center about five miles down the highway.

Carly excused herself to the ladies' room while he made arrangements to have the two flats repaired.

Standing in front of the wavy mirror, Carly saw her worst fears realized. Her hair was beginning to dry in strings, and mascara was running from the corners of her eyes. It was a wonder Dex hadn't fled, screaming.

Opening her purse, she set to work to repair the damage.

"It's going to be a couple of hours," he told her when she emerged fifteen minutes later. "I'm starving. Let's have a hamburger while we're waiting."

"Sure." She'd had dinner plans with Hayden, but he would understand if she canceled.

"Do you have a quarter I can borrow?" she asked.

Dex fished inside his pocket and came up with the change. He leaned against the wall, waiting patiently while she called Hayden and broke another date.

Laying his hand on the small of her back, he steered her through the glass doors adjoining the station.

"What'd you do to yourself? You look better."

She glanced up with a warning look. "Are you asking for it?"

"Are you offering it?"

The small diner was full of truckers. Some were eating while others lingered over their fourth cup of coffee, smoking Camels and listening to Reba McIntyre grieve over whoever was in New England with her man.

Sliding into an empty booth, Carly and Dex picked up menus and began to browse through the selections.

"I hope I'm not keeping you from anything?" Carly said. With the possible exception of Mireille, which really wouldn't bother her at all.

"No, I didn't have anything planned tonight. Look, they have BLTs," he said, remembering her fondness for that particular sandwich.

"Yeah, I saw that." Bread, a hundred calories, bacon, a hundred forty, mayonnaise . . . forget it.

Carly frowned, noticing that her finger was stuck to the menu. She discreetly pried it loose, then closed the menu and wedged it back between the napkin holder and the salt and pepper shakers.

"What are you having?" Dex asked.

"A dinner salad."

"Don't you ever eat anything worth eating?"

"Yes—and it's all in my hips. Want to see?"

He glanced up, his gaze measuring her leisurely. "Sure, why not?"

"Because it might upset Mireille." Ha!

"I doubt it. Mireille and I have an open relationship."

"Dex!"

He glanced up. "What?"

"An open relationship?" She'd noticed some changes in him, but nothing so drastic. He had always frowned on such arrangements.

He changed the subject. "Where's old Dinkler tonight?"

"Home, and stop calling him that. His name is Hayden, and he's really very nice. I called him to come and rescue me, but he was tied up in court."

"Ahhh. Too bad."

The waitress walked up, ready to take their orders.

"Two BLTs, two orders of fries, a large Coke, and a glass of skim milk." Dex nodded toward Carly. "The milk's for her. She's on a diet."

Carly just looked at him as the waitress walked away. "I wanted a small salad."

"No, you didn't. You wanted the BLT and fries."

"See!" She lowered her voice when she saw several sets of eyes swivel in her direction. "That makes me mad. You always override my decisions."

"Because what you say and what you mean are

two different things," he said patiently. "And speaking of which, if my correcting your errors bothered you so damn much, why didn't you say something about it?"

The conversation was about to take a serious turn. They had regressed a year. They were no longer talking about sandwiches.

"I tried to—you just never listened."

She could see by the way he reached for a napkin, jerking it angrily out of the dispenser, that her answer annoyed him. "The hell you did."

Folding her hands calmly on the table, she looked at him. His attitude puzzled her. This was the most emotion he had shown during the whole agonizing breakup.

One long year, and he was finally to the point where he was jerking napkins *angrily* out of holders.

Well, big deal. She'd done that for months. "I tried to explain, Dex."

"You did not."

"I did—why do you think I broke up with you?" At the time he'd never even bothered to ask!

"You said you didn't want to be engaged to me any longer."

Their eyes met and held for an uncommonly long time. Hurt mirrored in both, but love was there, too, strong and overriding.

"And you weren't the least bit puzzled about why?" she countered.

"I think you made it clear enough. You said you weren't sure that you wanted to spend your life with a man like me—whatever the hell that was supposed to mean. You said you were breaking the engagement. I didn't see that I had any choice."

"You could have questioned my decision."

"You didn't say, 'Dex, I've been thinking. I seem to be having these doubts—just little ones, mind you, nothing earthshaking, but I was thinking that maybe we should give ourselves a little more time—maybe not see so much of each other for a while—a few weeks—just long enough to give me some breathing space.' " He paused. "You didn't say that, Carly. You said, 'I'm breaking the engagement, Dex. Let's keep it clean and uncomplicated.' "

"Well, boy, you took me at my word," she accused him.

"Well, boy, that's what I was expected to do, wasn't it?"

The conversation halted as the waitress returned with their drinks. When she walked away, Carly asked softly, "Then why didn't you"— she wanted to use the term *love*, but resisted— "think enough of me to at least demand an explanation?" That was what had bothered her the most. He had just calmly accepted her decision and wished her good luck.

Good luck!

Dex drew a deep breath, stretching his damp shirt across his chest. He really hadn't changed much, Carly decided. Just . . . mellowed, maybe.

He wasn't quite as bossy, not quite so demanding, yet still a man with a purpose.

And he still had the power to make her heart race with just a quirk of a smile.

"You wanted freedom, Carly. I gave it to you."

"I'm not sure whether I should thank you or put a hex on you."

He smiled, and she thought the smile looked a little sad. "I think you've done both."

The sandwiches arrived, but they had both lost their appetites. After a few bites they half-heartedly pushed their plates back.

"What do you think about David's work?" Dex asked in an attempt to lighten the subject.

Carly shrugged. "Adequate."

Dex turned to watch the raindrops trickling down the window. "There's an opening coming up in my department. Do you think he would be better suited for marketing?"

"It depends on what he'd be doing. He's good with facts and figures." She toyed with her glass of milk. "But he's the only shortstop I've got."

Dex grinned.

She picked up a napkin and tossed it at him. "I'm warning you, Dex, take David away from me before the game, and you're dead meat."

He pitched the napkin back at her. "Whoooa, big mama. I'm quaking in my boots."

Someone got up and plugged another quarter into the jukebox. Sliding out of the booth, Dex held out his arms to her.

Reba McIntyre and Vince Gill were doing the

Oklahoma swing as they stepped onto the small dance floor.

Carly went into his arms as easily as if she had never left. After all, they weren't doing anything wrong; it was only a dance, she told herself. What was a simple dance between friends?

At first they held themselves apart a proper distance. They had the floor almost to themselves.

The truckers began to clap as the handsome couple did a lively two-step accompanied by sprightly twin fiddles.

A clap of thunder shook the small café. The lights flickered, and it poured buckets outside the truck stop, but nobody seemed to care. By now all the customers inside the diner were clapping their hands and stomping their feet in time to the music.

Whirling around the floor, Carly and Dex began to ham it up for the audience. They hadn't danced together in over a year, but they didn't look out of practice.

Around and around they twirled, laughing, colliding at times, keeping rhythm with the rowdy music.

When the song ended, the crowd came to its feet, giving Carly and Dex a standing ovation.

Red-faced and out of breath, they grinned at each other.

Clasping hands, they stepped to the middle of the floor, each taking a dramatic bow.

Turning back to each other, they kissed,

spurred on by the boisterous whistles and cat calls.

"You're still good, babe," Dex whispered against her lips.

"Thanks," Carly whispered back. And she meant it.

An hour later they were on their way back to Carly's car, two perfectly patched flats resting in the back of the Corvette.

Carly was thankful to find her Camaro still sitting beside the road with its rear end jacked up. In Chicago one could never be sure.

In his usual efficient manner, Dex had the tire back on the car, the spare in the trunk, and the tools packed away within minutes.

The rain had slackened momentarily, but the occasional flash of lightning in the east promised that the storm wasn't over.

"Well, that should do it." Dex walked back to the front of the car, wiping his hands on his handkerchief.

"I don't know how to thank you." Actually, she knew how she'd like to thank him, but it would be a little forward on her part. She smiled. "You've saved me twice this week."

"Twice?"

"Yeah, the incident in your office involving the T-shirt?"

He grinned, recalling the awkward moment. "Oh, yeah, the T-shirt."

They stood looking at each other, remembering.

Clearing her throat, Carly tried to smooth the wrinkles out of her skirt. It was still damp from the earlier soaking. "I need to get out of these clothes."

"My house is close," he offered.

Carly tried to swallow the knot that sprang to her throat. Dex was leaning against her car, arms crossed, watching her.

Thunder rumbled in the distance, and she knew what he was thinking. Rainy nights always put Carly in the mood for romance.

"How about it?" he prompted her lazily.

"No, thanks." He and Mireille might have an open relationship, but Carly didn't do things that way.

"It's going to rain all night." He cocked his head to one side. "Rainy nights? Soft music? Old movies?"

"Mireille?"

"She's in the hospital. Hayden?"

"Wouldn't like it."

Sliding behind the wheel of her car, she managed to still her wildly beating heart. Hospital! Mireille was in the hospital and he was inviting her home with him! He was perverted.

Perverted or not, she was still in love with him. She was tempted to accept his invitation. One night—one more gloriously unexpected night in his arms, making love . . .

She was a terrible person. Mireille's in the hospital!

So what if Mireille's in the—hospital, she argued with herself. They couldn't have too much of a relationship if he was inviting old girlfriends home on rainy nights.

No! Can't you see what he's doing? He was just toying with her. He saw the desire in her eyes, and he knew that she was still in love with him. What better revenge for her breaking the engagement than to take her to bed, then kiss her good-bye in the morning. Forever.

No, Dex wasn't like that! He wouldn't do anything so debased just to prove that she was wrong and he was right.

Dex is a man, honey. Sure, he acted as if he took the breakup calmly, but inside he was a smoldering mass of hostility. Women don't just break off with men like Dex Matthews and get away with it!

Dex rested his elbows inside the open window, his gaze meeting hers again. "You sure you won't change your mind?"

"Really, Dex." She meant to sound more conde-scending, but she found it hard to breathe with him so near.

He reached out, laying his finger on her cheek. "I can't think of anyone I'd rather spend the night with."

"Dex . . . I can't."

"Why?"

"Because."

"You and Dinkler serious?"

"No—I mean yes." She couldn't think straight.

'Yes?"

"No, no! I mean we're just dating, Dex." She had to get out of there!

Starting the car, she pulled it into gear. "Thank you for helping me. Maybe I can return the favor sometime."

Dex jumped clear as she suddenly gunned away in a shower of gravel.

Jamming his hands into his pockets, he watched the taillights of the Camaro merge into traffic, wondering why he found her refusal so damned disappointing.

Five

When the alarm went off Saturday morning, Carly rolled out of bed, showered, then put on shorts, an old sweatshirt, and tennis shoes.

Yawning, she headed for the kitchen, not particularly looking forward to the bowl of Special K awaiting her. Special K was fine if you wanted to look good in a white bathing suit, but Carly had never looked good in a white bathing suit, so why bother?

Trying to keep her eyes open, she rummaged in the cabinet for the box of cereal. She'd spent hours trying to find her catcher's mitt, so it had been after one before she'd gone to bed the night before.

She had finally found the obstinate glove in a box of miscellaneous paraphernalia she'd shoved into the back of her closet three years before. It had taken her another thirty minutes to loosen up the dried, cracked leather.

Slumped over the bowl, she halfheartedly spooned cereal into her mouth, dreading the double practice today.

Dex had suggested it would be good for the teams to practice together, just to give each other some good ol' competition, he'd said, and Carly had foolishly bought the idea.

She heard that the marketing team was *bad*—a bit of news that bolstered her spirits. Later she'd been informed by Matty Garrison, whose fourteen-year-old daughter knew everything, that in this case *bad* meant good, so the idea of the two teams practicing together didn't make a whole lot of sense, except to Dex. Once again he could prove his ability to best her without half trying.

But since she had already committed, she felt she was stuck with going through with it.

The whole idea of the softball game was idiotic. Just once she wished she could be around Dex without having to compete with him.

Hadn't her feelings of inadequacy already cost her an engagement?

Did she need to be reminded over and over again that she could have been married to Dex if she hadn't felt so threatened and insecure? If it hadn't been for her crazy need to compete with him, she would be the one in his bed mornings, not that slice of French toast, Mireille.

Realizing what she was doing, she shoved Dex

out of her mind for the hundredth time that week, dumped the remainder of the cereal into the disposal, and flipped on the switch. She didn't know how she was expected not to think about Dex Matthews when she bumped into him everywhere she went.

Hayden pulled into the drive and honked as she was spitting out the last mouthful of toothpaste. Rinsing her brush under the water, she pursed her lips in the mirror, checked her makeup again, then pitched the brush on the counter and ran.

It was close to nine when they arrived at the ball field.

The sun was out, robins were chirping, and a nice southerly breeze ruffled the large American flag, where below, a colorful bed of crocus and jonquils were blooming their little hearts out.

Spring had finally come to winter-weary Chicago.

Cars began pulling into the lot. Grumpy-looking coworkers dragged out of the cars, still sipping from cups of strong convenience-store coffee.

Carly thought they were showing about as much enthusiasm as a cat on his way to be neutered.

"All right, you guys! Heads up!"

She received a fair share of resentful looks, not to mention all the grumbling she heard as the players dumped their gym bags onto the bleachers, then sat down and began to put on their cleats.

Carly sighed and surveyed the motley assortment of players. Four or five men were wearing ragged cut-off shorts with T-shirts that hit them about mid-hairy-belly. The women wore sweats or shorts and oversize shirts—with the exception of Greta.

Greta had on a pair of magenta tights, hot-pink running shorts, a form-fitting top, with a matching magenta and hot-pink headband.

Carly could hear the men's teeth aching. Hank Johnson had already tripped over a bat and nearly broken his fool neck trying to get a closer look at "headlights."

"Is this thing going to be over by two?" Jim McGrady whined.

"I don't know, Jim, just get out there and warm up," Carly said. She felt her pulse kick into double time as Dex's car pulled into the lot.

A moment later he got out, dug around in the back of the Corvette, and emerged with huge bag filled with bats and balls.

Carly watched as he walked toward her with the heavy bag slung over his shoulder, thinking that it wasn't possible, but she could swear that he had gotten better-looking during this past year.

She liked the way his jeans hugged his thighs snugly and his gray-blue sweatshirt made his eyes look even bluer. Only the ball cap seemed a little out of character. She squinted, then frowned as she read the slogan:

BALL PLAYERS DO IT IN THE DIRT

Jeez.

Dropping the bag of equipment at her feet, Dex took off his hat, slicked back his hair, then settled the cap back onto his head. "What's happenin'?"

"Not much." But she felt sure that was about to change.

He turned sideways, adjusting his cap again as he surveyed the two teams. "Are we about ready to get the show on the road?"

Carly saw his gaze center briefly on Greta, then discreetly move on.

"I think so . . . Mireille didn't come with you this morning?" she asked nicely.

"No, she's still in the hospital."

"Oh . . . nothing too serious, I hope. I'm looking forward to meeting her."

"Naw, she's okay. A little female problem. She'll get over it." His gaze located Hayden, who was busy leaning bats against the backstop. "Who's that?"

"Hayden." She smiled, feeling terrifically smug. She was just darn glad that she wasn't the one in the hospital with the little female problem. Dex's concern was touching. "He came with me this morning."

"How nice." He tugged on the brim of his hat, then whistled for his team to take the field.

Turning back to her, his gaze leisurely swept the pair of denims she was wearing. Carly knew the extra pounds made them a little snug in the old keister, but they were decent. Her chin lifted defensively.

If he said one word about those few measly extra pounds, he's had it.

His brows rose. "What?"

"Don't say it," she warned him.

He grinned a grin that was so sexy, she felt the warmth of it spreading throughout her body. Without a word he turned and ambled out onto the field.

Four of the marketing team people were tossing balls back and forth while others were shagging grounders being hit to them.

Carly finally decided on her lineup and signaled Dex that she was ready for the practice to get under way.

"Batterrrr up!"

Greta was on the mound, preening, as Carly squatted behind the plate. She was adjusting her catcher's mask when she caught sight of Hayden and Dex standing at the fence. They had their arms looped over the chain-link fence, chatting like old confidants.

Eyeing the two men resentfully, she spit, wiped her mouth with the back of her hand, then flipped the mask shield back into place.

Great.

Why would Hayden strike up a conversation with his girlfriend's ex-fiancé?

Sometimes Hayden was just plain dense.

"Throw the ball!" she yelled at Greta.

Greta looked up from examining her manicure. "Now?"

"No, next Wednesday, Greta."

A moment later the ball thumped solidly into Carly's glove.

"Great." Carly sprang to her feet, surprised. That wasn't bad! "Gimme another."

Greta threw a few warm-up pitches—all fairly decent. Finally, Carly sent Brian into the box to see what he could do.

"Hey, batterr, batterrrr, batterrr," Carly shouted.

Brian shot her a knock-it-off look, then swung. He fouled the first ball off the bat, smacking Carly squarely in the chest.

The impact knocked her flat on her bottom.

Stunned, she sat in the dirt for a minute, trying to orient herself.

When it looked like she was parked for the day, Dex finally cupped his hands to his mouth and yelled, "Batter up!"

Crawling onto her knees, she retrieved the ball and threw it back to Greta.

Smack!

Carly fell forward, biting the dirt face first.

Hayden straightened. "Are you all right?" he called from the fence.

"Fine," Carly muttered, spitting the grit out of her mouth. "Just ducky."

Brian glanced back apologetically. "Sorry, I wasn't watching the ball." He dug in deeper, squaring the bat more firmly on his shoulder.

"Keep your eye on the ball, Brian," Carly urged, then squatted and braced herself. Mask or no mask, she had no desire to have every tooth in her head knocked out.

Her knees killed her as she balanced on her toes in the dirt, waiting for the throw again. She hadn't gotten around to working out signals with Greta, so she had to depend on the throw to be accurate.

Pop! The ball landed solidly in the mitt.

Bounding to her feet, Carly gave Greta the thumbs-up. "Awwwwright!"

Glancing Dex's way, she sent him a smug grin.

Eat your heart out, Dexy baby.

Unfortunately, Greta's ability to get the ball in the catcher's mitt was the highlight of the practice. From that point on, the game went downhill.

For the next hour Carly concentrated on evaluating the strength of each player which, in the end, wasn't hard to do. There were no strengths. Everyone stank.

After three batters attempted to hit flies to the infield, then the outfield—then to any field, Carly gave up and finally took possession of the bat herself.

Loyal Brown stumbled and fumbled around at shortstop for over thirty minutes. The ball either went through his legs, hit a clod of dirt and bounced, hitting him in the chest, or he tripped over second base.

Carly moved Loyal to right field and Morris Bellow to short—at least Morris had a shot at getting the ball back to home plate from there, since he'd seemed powerless to move it from right field to first base.

Edsel was on third base, and he hadn't caught the ball yet. He was good on chatter, though, so Carly left him where he was for the moment.

Shane was playing first. He wasn't all that bad, but Carly detected one inconsistency. Any time a ball was thrown or hit in Shane's direction, his foot left the bag, assuring the runner of a base hit.

The women weren't exactly scout material either. Dana, in left field, was more concerned about her hairdo than the ball. Carly just hoped no one could hit anything out that far.

Naturally, Dex's team was as smooth as a baby's bottom. The players moved fluidly around the field, jumping, stretching, bounding, and rebounding in perfect symmetry.

Even Becky Tharp, a cute blonde who always looked like she'd just stepped out of a department store window, was shagging grounders and throwing like a pro.

It wasn't fair. Carly had seen Becky reduced to tears over a chipped nail!

When Dex fell to his knees, beating the ground and heehawing like a jackass over a particularly embarrassing play by her team, Carly shot him a look that singed his eyelashes.

In the end it was Greta who provided Carly with her only hope. Strangely enough, Greta had a fast ball that matched anything Dex's pitcher could throw. She even had a riser or two that kept the men fascinated.

Now, if there were only a way to keep her out of that blasted T-shirt!

At two-thirty Carly wiped the sweat off her face with the tail of her shirt, her gaze returning to Dex and Hayden again. Their eyes were glued to Greta as she performed some totally unnecessary stretching exercises on the mound.

"Matthews, you're batters up!!" she yelled, hoping to break up the show.

By three o'clock everyone was worn out.

"Have a heart, Carly. Call it a day!" more than one disgruntled voice pleaded.

"Pantywaists," Carly grumbled. She was filthy, dripping with sweat, starving, and they were complaining.

"A ball game will be such fun!" Martin had said. Carly had had abscessed teeth she'd enjoyed more.

"Okay, guys—Monday night right after work!" she yelled as they broke for the bleachers in a mad frenzy. They were showing more enthusiasm running to the water fountain than they'd shown at any time during the practice!

Hayden began gathering equipment as Carly unbuckled her knee pads and let them drop to the ground. When the line at the water finally dwindled, she went over and took a long, cool drink.

Ducking her head under the spigot, she doused herself well. Straightening, she spotted Dex standing near the bleachers, looking over his lineup list. She snatched another hurried drink, then casually ambled his way.

Collapsing a-straddle on the cement bench, she lay back, staring at the clear blue sky. She realized that she looked so awful she shouldn't let him see her this way, but at the moment she didn't care. She'd come to the practice looking pretty snappy, but after couple of hours of rolling in the dirt she'd been forced to pull her hair back into a ponytail. Dragging the catcher's mask off and on every two minutes had resulted in pieces stringing loose, and the rest was either in a knot or standing straight up, stiff with dirt and sweat.

"Fun, huh?" Dex didn't look up as he continued to write on the clipboard he was holding.

"A real blast." She was grimy, sweaty, tired, and completely disgusted.

Straddling the bench opposite her, he watched as she undid her ponytail and shook out the dust. "Your team needs a little work," Dex commented as he laid the clipboard aside.

"No kidding." She sat up, surveying him sourly. He was still clean.

Dex grinned. Peeling back the wrapper on a Snickers bar, he offered her some. "Bite?"

"Are you asking or offering? If you're offering, I'm warning you, I'm going straight for the jugular vein."

His eyes glinted mischievously. "Whatever pops your corn."

She reached out, plucking the candy bar from his fingers. Closing her eyes, she took a bite, letting the heavenly rich chocolate slide over her tongue. Sighing, she handed it back to him.

Lifting the bar to his mouth, he took a bite, his gaze still locked with hers. She wasn't sure if he deliberately put his mouth exactly where hers had been or not, but it sure looked that way. She suddenly felt hot again.

Tossing pride aside, she sighed, lying back again. "Well, what do you think?"

"About your team?"

"Yeah."

"It stinks."

She sighed again. "Ain't it the truth."

"You sure they even know what game they're supposed to be playing?"

She reached for the candy bar again. Their fingers brushed, and Carly warned her pulse to stop it. It was ridiculous the way it acted when he was around.

Taking a large bite, she tried to control the string of rich, chewy caramel with the tip of her tongue. "What do you think my options are?"

"Two come to mind: leave town or commit suicide."

"I've considered both."

The candy bar changed hands, then back to Carly again.

"This is heavenly."

Dex eyed the dwindling bar anxiously. "You want one?"

"No, thanks. I'm on a diet." She handed the bar back to him, sighing again.

"Well"—he divided the last bite, handing her the biggest piece—"I can tell you from experience, leaving town won't help."

Carly could feel a thread of tension now. She turned her head, her gaze meeting his. "You didn't have to leave town."

The words hung between them like a heavy mist. Carly would have preferred that her tone sound more censuring because he hadn't had to leave town a year before. He could have stuck around for a while—at least until she'd had time to think about her reckless decision.

She knew that at the time he had been disillusioned with her, but hadn't they agreed to part friends? When she heard that he had moved to San Jose, she had cried herself to sleep that night. He hadn't even bothered to call her and say good-bye.

"You wanted time." Leaning forward, he casually slid the last bite of candy into her mouth. "I gave it to you."

How easily I could let myself believe that he's still in love with me. How incredibly easy it would be for me to ask for that love again.

"Well . . . maybe you shouldn't have." Carly reached out, trailing her finger over the familiar lines and planes of his face. For a moment it was easy to forget that he wasn't hers anymore. It seemed natural, so right to touch him. "You've never had any trouble telling me when I was wrong. Why didn't you stop me?"

Dex caught her hand and held it for a moment.

They gazed into each other's eyes, and Carly knew that he was about to kiss her.

Should she permit it? Hayden was off some- where, ogling Greta . . . but, no, it wouldn't be right.

Though her relationship with Hayden would never be anything more serious than an occa- sional date, she had more class than to permit one man to kiss her when she was technically with another.

Even if she was head over heels in love with that one man.

Dex moved closer, and she sighed, wondering where she would find the strength to stop him. She wanted him to kiss her . . . ached for him to kiss her, and she could see by the look in his eye that he intended to kiss her.

He lowered his head, his lips only inches from hers now. "Carly," he said softly, "there's some- thing I've been wanting to do all day."

She gazed up at him, her eyes growing warm and liquid. "Dex . . . remember Mireille," she warned. "And Hayden."

"Why?" he returned huskily. Their breaths mingled warmly, sending shivers down her spine.

"Because . . . " He was making it impossible for her to think. His mouth was so close . . . so ach- ingly close.

"This has nothing to do with Mireille and Hay- den. This is just between you and me."

"Dex . . . please." This was agonizing. How was

she going to prevent him from kissing her when she wanted it as badly as he did?

She reached out, trying to push him away, but he grabbed her hand and held it to his chest tightly. "Carly—"

She was a spineless jellyfish when he looked at her that way, all soft and wanting, and she knew she was going to give in to him.

Wrapping her arms around his neck, she gazed back at him. "All right. Do it."

Gazing back at her, he calmly plucked a stick out of her hair. "You've had this stuck in your hair for hours."

Carly bolted up, glaring at him.

Hayden's calling to them was the only thing that saved Dex from an instant, painful death.

Grinning at her, Dex waved to Hayden. "Be right there!"

The three walked toward the parking lot, carrying the equipment bags. Hayden and Dex struck up an amiable conversation, leaving Carly to straggle along behind them.

Greta saw them coming and waved. "We're going for pizza! Want to join us?"

Carly glanced at Hayden expectantly.

"Okay by me," he offered.

"I really should go home and clean up first," Carly fretted, shooting Dex another scathing look.

By now they had reached the cars, where a group from the office stood talking.

"Clean up? Huh-uh," Greta said. "Nobody else is going to clean up."

Nobody else looked as if she had been wallowing in a pigsty all afternoon.

Looping her arm through Dex's, Greta winked. "Come on, Coach. I'll buy you a pizza with everything on it."

Including the key to her apartment, Carly thought resentfully as she hurriedly turned from the sight of Dex walking off with his arm looped through Greta's.

Pitching her gym bag into the trunk of her car, she balanced on the end of the bumper and removed her cleats, wondering why Dex had purposely made her think he was going to kiss her.

Her cheeks flamed when she thought of the way she'd fallen for his little con game.

She glanced up to see Greta getting into the passenger side of his Corvette. Jealousy, hot and painful, flooded her, and she found herself biting back tears.

You're just tired, Carly. Don't let him get to you.

"Ready?" Hayden asked as he stowed the last of the gear inside the trunk.

"Ready."

She pulled herself off the bumper and got into the car, wondering why she suddenly felt more like a woman on her way to the guillotine than to a pizza parlor.

Six

Thursday morning the halls were buzzing with the scuttlebutt about the opening in marketing. Carly had found the rumors upsetting ever since the conversation she'd had with Dex while they were waiting for the tires to be repaired. She assumed that David would be the likely candidate for the position.

She made a mental note to ask Dex about that later and to remind him that David was her only shortstop.

Later that morning during a meeting, Carly heard speculation that Greta was interested in applying for the job, and a new, even more disturbing thought came into her mind.

Though it wasn't surprising, the scuttlebutt had served to make Carly feel edgy. Everyone knew that Greta had expressed a desire to move into marketing, and no one could argue that she wasn't qualified for the position. But suppose Greta did apply for the position—and got it. Jeez. Carly would rather lose David, her only shortstop, than Greta, her only pitcher!

Not only would the move mean that Greta would be working with Dex, which Carly suspected was Greta's primary goal, but it would screw up Carly's roster.

"Guess what?" Janis popped her head into Carly's office doorway later that morning.

"What?" Carly returned, her thoughts still involved with the research data she was studying.

"Greta's having lunch with Dex."

"Oh?" Carly replied. Calm, Carly. Calm! It shouldn't matter who Dex is having lunch with, should it?

Janis lowered her voice. "They're placing bets in the halls: Will Greta sleep with Dex for the job? Has she already? Will she get it? Did he get it—frankly, I'm betting that he didn't. How much can I put you down for?"

"Not one red cent!" Carly slammed the folder shut irritably.

"Oh, come on," Janis chided Carly. "Surely you don't think Dex would hire Greta because she's good at her job, do you?"

Carly shrugged. "I don't know what Dex would do, but Greta hasn't got the job . . . yet. David Honeycutt is qualified too, and I happen to know that Dex respects his work."

"Yeah, but David isn't built like Greta, Maybe

I'd better go through the old applications," Janis said, "just in case lust beats out ability." She frowned, realizing that Carly was taking the news well for someone who had once been engaged to Dex Matthews. "Doesn't it bother you? The fact that Greta and Dex will be putting in a lot of time together?"

"No, why should it?"

"There isn't some little—oh, you know—spark still smoldering between the two of you?"

Carly just plain lied. "Nope. We're good friends, and I like it that way. So does he."

"Oookay," Janis drawled. "But I'll just take a look at those applications anyway."

"You do that," Carly said shortly, opening the research folder again.

As the door closed, she tried to regain her concentration, but Dex's face kept superimposing itself on the pages until she finally shoved the work aside irritably.

Taking an early lunch, Carly accompanied Joanne, a friend from research, to the deli. They ordered sandwiches and found a small table in the corner. Joanne didn't take long in coming around to the tidbit of the day.

"I hear Greta's moving up to marketing."

"So I've heard." Every time I turn around.

"What do you think?"

"I think nothing is set in stone yet. Has it ever occurred to anyone that there might be others at Montrose who might be considered for the opening?"

"Ha." Joanne picked up her sandwich and bit into it morosely. "If 'Boobs' Schmidt wants the job, it's hers."

"If you'll recall, Greta was hired in research with the understanding that her first love was marketing," Carly reminded her friend.

Joanne eyed Carly over the rim of her coffee cup. "First love was marketing or was *in* marketing?"

"Oh, Joanne, not you too!" Carly groaned. "Will someone give Dex a little credit? He's already involved with a woman—why would he be wanting to fool around with Greta?"

Joanne's brows rose in disbelief.

"Dex isn't interested in Greta." Carly held firm to her belief that Dex hadn't completely lost his mind. "He isn't like that."

"Pooh. All men are like that—has something to do with the power of personal persuasion and the size of one's assets."

"Double pooh. I happen to think that all men aren't like that . . . and the day Dex Matthews is persuaded to hire an employee based upon the size of her bustline is the day I'll tattoo his name across my butt!"

"Ummmm," Joanne murmured, trying to picture the intriguing scenario. "Interesting."

Fortunately, Joanne let the topic drop, but the suggestion that Dex would actually hire Greta on such an unprofessional basis wouldn't leave the fringes of Carly's mind.

Carly, give him a break. He just took Greta to lunch as a formality. He won't actually hire her.

That afternoon the word came down the pipe: Greta was moving to marketing.

The announcement hit Carly with the force of a bullet train.

After disappearing into the bathroom, she lost her lunch and hated herself for having so little control over her emotions.

Later, she leaned weakly against the counter, running a wet paper towel across her face.

You've got it bad, kiddo. Real bad.

With sinking clarity she realized that she could no longer pretend that Dex didn't still have a strong effect on her . . . because he did.

Now it was a matter of figuring out a way to live with it.

"Hi! Got a minute?"

"Sure," Carly glanced up just before five to find Greta standing in the doorway. "Come in."

Motioning for Greta to be seated, Carly wondered if she was there to gloat or to apologize. Foolishly, she prayed for the latter.

"You've probably heard . . . Dex and I had lunch together," Greta began.

"I did hear something along those lines."

"He offered me a position in marketing."

"I see."

"I accepted."

Carly fought the spurt of anger that shot through her, determined to remain civil. Clearing her throat, she rose, picked up the manila folders, and walked to the metal file cabinet. "Well, I appreciate your coming to me in person. I'm aware that you've wanted to move to marketing for some time, and it's nice that something finally worked out for you."

"You're not upset?"

"Upset? Of course not. You've made no secret of having an interest in marketing, and it's all a part of the reorganization." Carly's 'happy face' was getting harder and harder to maintain. Darn you, Dex, why did you have to screw everything up this way! "I hope you aren't planning on leaving immediately."

"Well . . . that's what I wanted to talk to you about. If you have no objections, Dex would like for me to report to marketing on Monday."

Carly whirled around to face Greta. Diplomacy be hanged! "Monday! You can't! That gives me only a few days to find another pitcher!"

"Pitcher!" Greta's face went blank. It was apparent to Carly that Greta hadn't considered her move in terms of the ball game. "Well, gee, I'm sorry . . . but Dex just thought . . ."

"Well, *Dex* can just cool it until after the ball game!" Carly fired back.

Giving her a "well, jeez, don't get out of shape" look, Greta eased out of her chair, hoping to make a clean break for the door. "Look, you and

Dex can talk about it, then let me know what I'm supposed to do? Okay?"

"Peachy!"

Thirty seconds after Greta had left her office, Carly went striding angrily down the hallway.

"Is he in?" Carly demanded, marching right past Dex's secretary's desk.

"Yes, but he doesn't want to be . . ." Toni said in a protective way.

"Is he alone?"

"Yes . . . but . . ."

"Hold his calls. He's going to be tied up for a little while."

The brunette grinned cheekily. "Oh, kinky stuff! I love it!"

Carly strode to Dex's door, opened it, and slammed it shut behind her.

Dex glanced up blankly.

"How dare you!" she demanded.

"Huh?"

"How dare you!"

"Yeah, I got that. How dare I what?"

"How dare you hire Greta right out from under me! She's my pitcher! You did this deliberately!"

"Your pitcher? I believe you've lost sight of our purpose, Carly. Montrose is a business, not a farm club."

Drawing herself up straighter, she stared at him coldly. "What happened to David?"

"I talked to David, and he said he didn't want

to make a move right now, so when Greta asked to—"

"Don't try to worm your way out of it! I know what's going on!"

Leaning back in his chair, Dex let her rant. "Okay, you know what's going on. Now tell me."

"All right, I will. You took Greta home from ball practice the other night—it was raining—" Her voice broke and she paused, drawing a deep, ragged breath. She hated it when she lost control in front of him.

"And?"

"And, naturally, after a night with 'Boobs' Schmidt—"

" 'Boobs' Schmidt?"

"That's right, don't deny it, you snake." Carly leaned forward, wagging her finger at him sternly. "You slept with her!"

Dex came to his feet, resting the palms of his hands flat on his desk. "I did not."

"You did so!"

"I did not."

"Don't lie, I know you did!"

The sound of his hand slapping the desk sounded like a thunderclap! "I did not, dammit!"

"Well"—Carly tossed her head haughtily—"not that it matters to me what you do, I just think it's pretty darn low for you to steal my only pitcher—but if winning the game means that much to you"—she dismissed the childish tactic airily—"then by all means take Greta."

"Will you calm down for a minute and tell me

what in the hell you're talking about?" he asked
calmly.

She whirled. "Greta!"

"What about Greta?"

"You've hired Greta—and you can't fool me—"
She thumped her chest. "I know why. Not only
do you want to make a fool of me on the ball field,
you've hired Boobs Schmidt to get back at me for
breaking our engagement! That's it, isn't it? Plain
and simple! Plain and simple! It's taken a year,
but you finally did it. Are you happy?"

Dex shook his head as he sat down. "Why
would I want to get back at you?"

"Because I broke our engagement!" Carly was
so consumed by guilt, she couldn't shut up. Once
started, she couldn't contain her frustrations.
She was mad! Mad at Dex, mad at the world, and,
most of all, mad at herself. She had no one to
blame but herself for the hell she'd endured during the past year, and yet she felt compelled to
make him suffer too.

Dex looked at her, a quirk of amusement forming at the corners of his mouth. "That's what you
think? That I've hired Greta as part of some sinis-
ter plot to get even with you for breaking our engagement?"

"Yes."

He snapped shut the manila folder before him,
his amusement gone. "I hired Greta because she
is the most suitable person for the job, and ball
game or no ball game, Ms. Winters, I've got a
department to reorganize and I damn well plan to

do it as competently and as efficiently as I know how—and I don't intend to explain my decisions to you, now or in the future."

Carly's bravado began to crumble. Turning her back to him and facing the window, she was appalled to feel hot tears streaming from the corners of her eyes. He had never talked to her this way before, never. "I don't have to defend a business decision to you, Carly," he added.

Carly's fury heightened another notch. "Well, of course. How stupid of me. You wouldn't do a simple thing like that because you *never* explained anything to me! That's what was wrong with our relationship. You always assumed I wasn't worthy of knowing your business!"

"No. You really want to know what was wrong with our relationship? This kind of kneejerk reaction to everything! You never stop to think! Did it ever occur to you to ask me what I had in mind when I hired Greta? No! You just assumed you knew."

"I'm usually right."

"There is room for improvement."

"See?"

"No, I don't see," he said vehemently. "I fail to see why our business affairs should interfere with our personal lives. If it upset you so damn much working with me, why didn't you say so? One of us could have changed jobs!"

"That's ridiculous. You wouldn't have changed jobs."

"I would have if it had meant the difference between keeping you or losing you."

Their eyes met, causing a large lump to form in Carly's throat.

"I loved you, Carly, and I did my damnedest to keep you happy. You know it and I know it," he said quietly.

"Maybe it seemed that way to you."

"Name me an instance that it wasn't."

"Peanut butter," Carly said, grabbing for an imaginary straw.

"Peanut butter?"

"You never had any. You knew I liked peanut butter, but you refused to buy some."

Stupid, Carly. Stupid!

"You told me not to! You were always on one of those diets! How was I supposed to know when to buy peanut butter and not get my head bitten off?"

"And socks," Carly challenged. "What about the socks?"

"What about my socks?"

"You never wore the ones I bought you. They weren't good enough for you."

"Come on, Carly. I wear dark socks to the office. Is that a crime?"

"No, you just have to be right and have me wrong."

"Wrong."

"Right!"

It seemed like old times.

"And what about my checkbook?"

"What about it? I had to balance it," he reminded.

"I didn't ask you to balance it! You just took over like everything else! Good ol' Mr. Fix-It! Whatever it was, Mr. Perfect could do it better."

Dex caught himself from smarting back. Was that all she'd ever seen in their relationship? His putting her down?

"Nothing I did was ever good enough." Tears began to roll unabashed down her cheeks. "You could always do it better, whether it was research or washing dishes. There was always a right way and a wrong way—or more specifically, Carly's way." Carly was sobbing now, but she couldn't stop. The past year had been sheer torture. "I just hated that . . . that . . . 'come on, stupid, this is a better way to do it' attitude you always had when we worked together. Like I was some . . . child!"

Dex's jaw firmed. "Carly . . ."

She began to sob harder, long, racking moans that tore at him. Reaching out, he drew her to him and held her tightly as she cried. "Dammit, Carly, don't do this . . ."

In a flash she was in his embrace, outraged that she was a woman of so little pride. All she wanted at that moment, or needed, was to let him hold her, to let him love her again.

Her fingers curled into the front of his shirt, and their mouths came together before they had time to think. Time ceased, as his lips, hot and demanding, took possession of hers.

The sensation was so sweet, so overpowering,

the blood in Carly's head pounded and she was caught in a blinding flash of heat. Desperately, he kissed her harder, and suddenly they couldn't hold each other close enough. Though Carly moaned in protest as much as in appreciation, she knew she would die if he stopped.

They were only vaguely aware of the door opening, and Toni's voice saying hesitantly, "Dex . . . I'm sorry, but Mr. Gathier is waiting. . . ."

When Dex drew away, Carly was dazed, her face flushed with heat. "Thanks, Toni, give me a minute, then send Jack in," he said quietly.

The door closed, and Carly looked at him.

"You okay?" he asked.

She nodded, not at all sure that she was or ever would be again. "I'd better go," she murmured.

Turning, she walked to the door, knowing she should say something more, but not able to think of a thing.

"Carly."

She turned, "Yes?"

"I didn't sleep with Greta, and I loved those damn socks you gave me. I guess I just never told you."

She sent him a sad smile. He was free to do what he wanted, but it was nice to know that he hadn't. "I guess maybe I should have asked."

Before he could say anything more, she left, closing the door behind her.

Seven

Being in love stank. Carly hid in her office the rest of the day, warning Janis that she didn't want to be disturbed for any reason. She'd planned to work on the research project for Powder Puff, but she just couldn't. When she discovered that she had been staring at one sheet for over an hour, she finally gave up. Her mind simply could not be concerned with "that feel fresh feeling all day."

Her argument with Dex kept turning over in her mind. How stupid it had been. What on earth had possessed her to bring up things like peanut butter and the color of his socks?

"Hi."

Carly jumped guiltily as Joanne stuck her head through the doorway. "Oh, hi."

"It's after five. Want to go for a drink? I'm beat."

"I don't know, Joanne." Carly glanced at her calendar, then frowned. Drats. She'd promised to go to a bar association dinner with Hayden that evening. She sighed, dreading the thought of another long, boring after-dinner speech. She couldn't do it, not tonight. "Oh, what the heck," Carly muttered. "Hold on a minute. I need to make one quick phone call."

"I'll meet you by the elevator. Five minutes?"

"Five minutes," Carly promised, then picked up the phone and dialed Hayden's number.

"Hi," she said when Hayden answered.

"Hi, I was just getting ready to call you."

"What's up?"

"I thought we might have a drink before dinner, so if you can be ready by seven—"

"Uh . . . Hayden."

A long pause followed, then, "Yes?"

"I hate to do this . . ."

There was another lengthy pause.

"Carly."

"Yes?"

"You're not going to break another date, are you?"

The nearly pathetic invocation in Hayden's voice tempted her to change her mind. So she would go to the stodgy dinner and be bored out of her mind. It wouldn't be the first time. "Well . . . not if the dinner's that important."

"Has something come up that will make it impossible for you to attend?"

"Well . . . Joanne just wanted me to have a

drink with her, and I have this ripping headache."

"Again? You seem to be having a lot of headaches lately, Carly. Maybe you should see a doctor."

"I'm fine, really. Things are just a little rough here lately, with the reorganization and all. And now I've lost one of my assistants, and I've got to find another in a hurry." One that can get a ball over home plate. "I just feel that I wouldn't be very good company tonight, that's all."

"Well, it will be a rather dry evening. Chub Wilcox is speaking," Hayden conceded, as if that alone were a viable reason for Carly to be excused. "Maybe I'll ask Jenny Witmer to go . . . she mentioned that she's been wanting to hear Chub speak."

Carly jumped at the reprieve. "That's a great idea! Jenny would probably love to go."

"Yeah . . . maybe" Hayden agreed. "But tomorrow night is extremely important to me, Carly . . . you do plan to come tomorrow evening, don't you?"

Carly glanced at her calendar again with a sinking heart. There was a political function scheduled, and she had agreed to accompany Hayden. "Sure, looking forward to it," she said brightly.

"Good, good. We'll have a great time."

Sure, sure. As great a time as one could have eating rubber chicken, dried peas, and tasteless mashed potatoes, followed by an equally dry speech about some environmental impact study up for review during the next legislative session, Carly thought.

She didn't know why she always agreed to go to these things with Hayden. She usually slept through the speeches with her eyes wide open, then after the applause died away, on cue she stood up and pasted a cardboard smile on her face while Hayden went around to each table, shaking hands and chatting amiably with the most influential in attendance.

Maybe Hayden was thinking of running for office. The thought made Carly's head pound harder.

"Well, make sure you take something for your headache. Shall I call you later?" For some reason, the way he invariably asked that question was beginning to irk her.

"No, I'm going to bed early," she said. "But you have a nice evening."

Reaching for her purse, she hung up, then headed for the elevator. Twenty minutes later she was sitting at a small table with Joanne in a downtown restaurant that specialized in Mexican food.

"Well, let's see." Carly studied the wine list. "I think I'll have a spritzer."

"Yeah, that sounds good."

They closed the menus, relaxing.

"I guess you've heard," Carly said.

"About Greta?"

"Yeah. Too bad."

"Yeah."

Carly toyed with the wine list, then casually opened it again.

"They say they have great margaritas here," Joanne mused.

"Ummm . . . no, margaritas are too strong for me."

They gazed at the menu, trying to decide.

"You know, maybe I'll have a small glass of white wine." She didn't drink too often, but maybe tonight she would relax her standards. The thought of Dex transferring Greta to his department bothered her, she couldn't deny that.

"Yeah, wine does sound good," Joanne said agreeably. "What are you going to do about replacing Greta?"

"I don't know . . . try to find someone with a background in research who can get a ball across home plate, I guess."

"Boy, that's going to be tough."

"Tell me about it."

Picking up the menu a third time, Carly studied it glumly. "You know . . . I'm suddenly in the mood for something stronger than wine. Maybe a mixed drink . . . what do you think?"

"Gee, I don't know." Neither woman drank very much, but after the trying day they'd had, a mixed drink sounded good. "Like what?"

"I don't know . . . what's schnapps?"

"I'm not sure . . . something fruity, I guess. There's peach, strawberry, blackberry . . ."

"Hmmm, probably couldn't be real strong if it has fruit in it."

"I wouldn't think so."

Closing the menu, Carly decided to try one. "Let's have a peach schnapps."

"Okay by me."

The waiter took their order and returned momentarily with their drinks in two shot glasses.

They fell silent as they sipped thoughtfully. Liquor usually gave Carly a headache, but today was different. Today Dex was back in her life, and she was certain one peach schnapps wasn't going to ease her discomfort. Pushing her empty glass aside, she signaled the waiter for another. The drink was strong, but quite refreshing.

Joanne started to protest, but Carly stopped her. "I'm still thirsty."

"But you don't drink . . ."

"Normally, no. I don't happen to think that drinking solves anything, but tonight I don't seem to give a wit. And these glasses are so small," she complained.

Shrugging, Joanne went back to work on her first drink.

"Dex knew Greta was the only team member I had who could even halfway play ball." Carly dunked a tortilla chip in salsa, then ate it. "There's no way I can find somebody to take her place before the game Saturday."

"Yeah, that's real dirty of him."

"The snake."

Carly doused another chip and ate it. She was beginning to feel a little light-headed.

"Well, maybe he's just trying to strengthen the two departments," Joanne offered. "You know he's real hardnosed when it comes to work."   .

The two fresh drinks arrived, and Carly washed the hot salsa taste from her mouth.

"You said you expected it to happen," Joanne went on. "Everyone knows Greta's been interested in marketing."

"And Dex."

"Yeah." Joanne reached for her second drink. "And Dex." A moment later she blinked, trying to clear her eyes. "Wow. Do these things seem strong to you?"

Lifting her head, Carly tried to focus on Joanne, who suddenly looked a little swimmy. " 'Course not. Let's order another."

"Gee, I don't know." Joanne leaned down, peering into the half-empty glass. "I still have enough left of this one."

Carly leaned over, peering into the glass with her. "Huh-uhhhh."

"Uh-huhhhh!"

Carly's hand flew out to clap across Joanne's mouth. "Shussssssss . . . some one'll hear us!"

Batting Carly's hand aside, Joanne giggled. "Maybe we should order sumpin' to eat . . . I think the schnapps is going straight to our heads."

"Oh . . . poo, we already have sumpin' to eat." Opening her mouth, Carly placed a tortilla chip on her tongue and wiggled it comically.

They both got tickled, dissolving into snickers. When Joanne noticed they were getting some odd looks, she cupped her hand to her mouth and whispered, "Shhhhh—now hear this. I think we're getting a li'l tipsy."

"Uh-huhhhhh!" Heads pivoted, and Carly snickered again, spraying corn-chip crumbs out onto the table. Embarrassed, she sheepishly fumbled for a napkin to scrape up the crumbs.

Bursting into giggles again, the two women lifted their glasses and slurped loudly.

"Think there's anything to the rumor 'bout Dex and Greta?" Joanne asked.

Carly caught the waiter's eye and ordered two more drinks. "Dunno for certain, but if I knew how to get hold of his girlfriend . . . Muriel . . . or whatever the heck her name is, I'd put a bug in her ear 'bout those rumors." Carly wagged her finger beneath Joanne's nose. "Bet ol' French toast'd let him know which side of the covers business decisions are supposed to be made on."

Joanne giggled. "Yeah, maybe we should leave her a little . . . a . . . anon . . . anonymous note."

"Yeah . . . maybe we should. Thas a good idea, buddy. That'll fix that ol' snake. Let's do it." Carly suddenly paused, squinting to see Joanne more clearly. "Joanne?"

"Yeah?"

"You drunk?"

"Nah. You?"

"Nah."

" 'Kay, I'll write the note so ol' what's-her-face can't accuse you," Joanne promised, draining her glass.

The thought of Dex with another woman hurt. Whether it was Mireille or Greta, it didn't matter. It just plain old hurt. Tears rolled down Carly's cheeks as she picked up her napkin and blew her nose. How could Dex have done this to her? Why did he have to come back and mess up her life this way? She'd been just about over him. "Darn snake's just a phil . . . phil . . . philanderer. And I'm gonna tell him so the next time I see him."

"Ahhh." Joanne leaned forward, patting Carly's hand consolingly. "It'll be all right. Greta probably can't interest Dex 'cause he's already in love with Murrreille," she finished brightly.

Carly's face clouded up like a spring storm.

"Ahhhh . . . don't cry," Joanne soothed. "No man's worth it."

While Carly blubbered, Joanne tried to focus on the hands of her watch. "Oh—will you look at that? It's six-thirty. I've gotta get home."

"Yeah . . . me too," Carly said, but couldn't remember why.

They managed to pay for their drinks and walk outside.

"Hey! Mr. Doorman!" Carly, feeling better now, put her fingers to her lips and whistled.

The valet stepped forward, "Yes, ma'am."

"We need some wheels," Carly said, rummaging inside her purse to locate her parking ticket. Her head was spinning like a top. She suddenly knew why she didn't drink much.

"Hey, wait a minute. Think I drove, I'm almost sure of it," Joanne said.

"You did?" Carly tried to think. "You sure, Joanne . . . you're not lying to me?"

They broke up giggling again.

"Ladies, may I call you a cab?" the valet inquired discreetly.

Carly tried to bring Joanne into focus. Her friend seemed to be weaving all around and grinning. Joanne was drunk, Carly thought disgustedly, drunk with a capital D.

Leaning toward the valet, Carly whispered, "Thank you, sir, I think my friend has had a litttllle tooo much to drink." She winked and elbowed the valet in his side as her perceptive gaze drifted to Joanne.

Stepping to the curb, the valet signaled for two cabs. A moment later he bent forward and helped Joanne into the first one.

"See you in the morning . . . if I make it," Joanne acknowledged. She leaned against the back of the seat, her head swimming.

"Bye." Carly lifted her hand, waving her fingers back at her friend. Then, on impulse, she leaned forward and goosed the valet.

The man shot up like a rocket.

Carly doubled over, laughing and slapping her hands on her thighs.

Eyeing her sourly, the valet opened the door of the second cab. "Your cab, madam."

Carly nodded regally. "Thank you, kind sir."

She was still snickering as she crawled onto the backseat. A second later she slumped to her side in a daze.

"Where to, lady?"

"Ummmm . . ." Now, where was she going? Oh, yes. She was going to give Dex Matthews a piece of her mind. He wasn't going to get away with stealing her pitcher. . . .

"Ma'am?"

"Take me to that street where that 'nake lives."

"Ma'am?" the cabbie repeated patiently.

She peered over the seat. "Gotta be more exact, huh?"

'Yes, ma'am."

Carly sighed. Boy, leave it to a man to complicate matters.

The doorbell continued to ring as Dex hurried to answer it. Some fool was leaning on the bell.

He opened the door to find Carly propped against the doorway, her finger still on the button.

"Outta my way, you fink." Carly waved him aside as she casually sauntered inside.

She paused, looking around. His apartment was nice, but she couldn't spot a hint of a woman's touch anywhere. Ol' Mireille must not be the domestic type.

She turned to look at Dex, who was still standing at the door, staring at her.

Covering her mouth, she began to giggle. He was barefoot, and wearing glasses—she'd never seen him in glasses before—and his perfect little silk tie was missing and his shirt collar was open. He actually looked a bit rumpled.

"Carly, what is going on?" He closed the door.

"Well, thas jus' too bad," she said flippantly, having not the slightest idea what he'd said.

She was drunk, Dex realized. In all the time he'd known her, he'd never seen her drunk, but she was now. Flat-out, smashed.

"I got somethin' to say to you, buster." Spotting the sofa, she began to weave her way across the room. *You're a little tipsy, Carly, ol' girl. Better sit yourself down.*

Aiming for the middle cushion, she missed and slid instead to the floor. She looked around, momentarily confused.

Dex came around the sofa to pick her up and set her on the couch.

It's all right, she would just be cool . . . he hadn't even noticed.

Carly primly adjusted her skirt, then glanced up, smiling. "Thanks."

"You need some coffee." He turned and started toward the kitchen when she stopped him.

"No coffee!" she blurted out. "This isn't a social call, buster. I got somethin' I wanna say to you." Kicking her shoes off, she leaned back, running her gaze over him from beneath her lowered eyelids.

"Carly, dammit, you're drunk."

"Me? Ha." She pushed her fingers through her hair, then adjusted her skirt so it was just above her knees.

There, Snake Matthews, get a loada them gams. Ol' Carly's legs—though admittedly a tinge large— are every bit as good as Greta's or Mireille's.

"Walll . . . maybe I had a little gallon of this fruity snots stuff—"

"Fruity what?"

"Snots. You ever drink any?"

"Not consciously."

"It's berry good." She laughed, amused by her own wittiness.

She ran her tongue over her lips sensuously, brushing one hand over the curve of her hip to gain attention.

Seeing her this way made Dex feel like a grade A, homogenized jerk. He should never have come back, he realized. He should have just walked away from the relationship and never looked back.

Their working together, their ball game, their agony of seeing each other every day, their watching each other live lives that no longer included the other—it was all as debilitating to her as it was to him.

Holding his hand out, he coaxed softly, "Come on, sweetheart, let me make you a cup of coffee—"

"Don't want no coffee," she wailed. "Want whiskey and water."

"Whiskey and what?"

"Whiskey and water," she repeated throatily.

There, she could be sophisticated and sexy too.

"Judas Priest!" Striding to the small bar, Dex

dumped ice into a glass, then filled it with club soda with a twist of lime. "How long have you been like this?"

"Like what?" Accepting the drink he handed her, she smiled smugly. "I can hol' my liquor well as anyone else. You'll see." She took a sip, her gaze refusing to leave his. "Perfect. Jus' the way I like it."

Holding her nose, she downed the rest of the drink, then held the glass out to him. "I'll have another, please."

"Carly . . ."

"Another!" she demanded.

Dex returned to the bar to pour another club soda with lemon.

"It's not fair, you know," she accused him.

Dex turned slightly, looking over his shoulder at her. "What's not fair?"

She slumped against the pillow, staring at her hands as if she'd never seen them before.

"You and Greta."

"Me and Greta." Dex sighed. So that was what had brought this on.

Carly forced herself to sit up and wag her finger at him. "You shouldn't have come back here, you snake. I was gettin' along jus' fine . . . then you had to come back. I don't need . . . need you back in my . . . my life."

"No, but maybe I need you back in mine," he returned quietly.

But Carly didn't hear him. She was so immersed in her misery that she couldn't hear or feel anything. She was numb. "I didn't . . . didn't want to still love you. I wanted to for . . . forget you . . . 'cause it hurts too darn much." Her gaze surveyed the bare finger on her left hand. "Gave your ring back . . . stupid, stupid, stupid!"

Easing onto the sofa, he attempted to take her into his arms, but she pushed him aside. Pain radiated from her eyes.

"I had to do it . . . don't you see? There was no other way. . . ."

"Let's make coffee, then we'll talk—"

Carly grasped the front of his shirt, bringing his face closer to hers. "I was ti-tired of competing with you. Everything I did, you could do better."

Oh Lord, Dex agonized. He hadn't meant for her to feel that way.

"Jus' once"—she held up two wobbly fingers—"jus' once, I wanted . . . I wanted to do something better than you. Jus' once, I wanted to do somethin' that you wouldn't pick apart."

"Carly, if I had known—"

"But I shouldn't have d-done it." Dex's handsome features swam before her as her fingers closed around his chin, trying to steady him. "You're so cute . . . when we were good together . . . remember?" She closed her eyes, memories washing over her. "So good . . ."

"Sweetheart—"

"And, ya see, you are better than me," she avowed. "That's what gets me. You win awards and write articles for *Forbes* . . . an' I jus' plug along . . . plug along, plug . . . plug . . . plug along jus' like always . . ." She sniffed, blinking furiously to keep back the tears. "Even Joanne said you're better'n me."

"Joanne said that?"

Carly nodded. Well, Joanne really hadn't said that—but that's what she'd thought. Carly was certain of it. "I was beginning to think maybe I could get over you being better than me . . . but I jus' can't." She eyed him enviously. "Snake. Never were happy with me."

"Look, I'm not the snake in this relationship. I was perfectly happy with you—and what the hell has Greta got to do with this? I told you this afternoon why I hired Greta."

Carly's head bobbed back and forth smugly. "Did not."

"Carly, I'm not going to argue about this. Greta is an employee. Nothing more."

"You hired Greta because she has a . . . a bigger . . . bigger b-bust . . . and now, because of you, I have to . . . to tattoo your name across my . . . my . . . b-buttttttt!" Carly dissolved in tears.

Groaning with frustration, Dex ran his hands through his hair as Carly hunched over, sobbing into her hands.

Reaching over, he pulled her into his arms and held her tightly against his chest. "Come on, Carly. You're making me crazy."

He gently smoothed her hair as she sobbed against his shoulder, her fingers twisting the front of his shirt into a tight knot.

A flood of memories washed over her: the time

her mother had been so seriously ill that she and Dex had sat up all night, holding each other's hands, the evening they'd celebrated their engagement when they'd purchased a bottle of Dom Pérignon, driven to the airport, stretched out on the hood of the car beneath a starry sky, and watched the flights come in.

She crawled closer to him, aware of the strong, steady beat of his heart against her palm. His shirt was halfway unbuttoned, and she could feel the hair-rough skin of his chest against her cheek. She loved him so much, so very, very, much.

"Carly . . . now . . . you're drunk and—"

"Poo, not drunk, jus' wanna feel you . . ." She gazed at him as her hand moved beneath his shirt and feathered over his skin. She smiled when she heard his breath catch. Burying her face in his neck, she pressed her lips against his warm skin. 'Ummm . . . smell so good . . ."

"Carly," he warned in a tone that had suddenly grown husky with desire.

Laying her hand on the front of his trousers, she patted him affectionately. "Missed you . . . missed you so much," she whispered brokenly. "Did you miss me?"

She wanted to hear him say it—it wasn't as if she were trying to take him away from Mireille— she just needed to hear him say that he had missed her as much as she had missed him.

"I think we should discuss this later," he said, trying to move her aside.

"Why?"

"You're not thinking straight."

"Am too—you think I'm bombed, don't you?"

"I think you need black coffee."

"Don't want coffee! I know what I'm saying."

Laying his shirt all the way open, she touched her tongue to his chest, then up to nuzzle his ear as she began to ease down the zipper on his trousers.

Tensing, Dex groaned softly as he buried his hands in her hair. He had to put a stop to this. It wasn't hard to see where she was heading. But as badly as he wanted her, he couldn't take her— not like this.

"Say you missed me," she coaxed, placing moist kisses across his lips, at the corners of his mouth.

"You know I did." His voice was incredibly deep and masculine, causing her heart to race wildly.

"Not bad enough," she whispered. Their mouths touched, their breaths mingling. His delicious scent fueled her, made her recklessly bold as his lips closed over hers slowly and hungrily.

Carly felt her bones melt as he kissed her face all over, quick kisses that took her breath away.

Returning to her mouth, Dex kissed her long and deep, aware that passion was momentarily overriding his common sense.

"Dex?"

"Ummm?"

"Could we go to the bedroom and jus' kinda lie down? I'm very tired."

"No. If we did that, I would want to make love to you."

"Oh? Well . . . maybe I would let you. That wouldn't be so awful, would it?"

"Depends. For instance, if we asked Hayden, he probably wouldn't like the idea," Dex said. She wasn't in love with Hayden, he knew that. He just wanted to make her aware of it.

"Hayden's eatin' chicken with Jenny."

They kissed again, hot and eagerly. His hands cupped her breasts, exploring her intimately as their mouths steadfastly refused to separate.

"Wanna go to bed with you," she whispered raggedly. "Wanna make love with you . . ."

The kiss suddenly became hotter, more urgent as she leaned against him, blindly seeking his love. It had been so long, so very long.

He moaned, gathering her into his arms. His mouth melded to hers as he stood and carried her toward his bedroom.

"Want you . . . want you so bad . . ." She kissed him on the eyes, the nose, the mouth. "Tell me you still love me," she pleaded, desperate to hear him say the words that had once come so easily for him.

"I still love you."

"No, say, 'I still love you, Carly, just you'—say it like that." She showered his face with passionate kisses as he walked through the bedroom, straight into the adjoining bath.

Propping her against the counter, he steadied her with one hand, while he opened the shower door and turned on the cold faucet with the other.

Carly wagged her finger at him. "Uh-uh, no shower. I want to—"

Her protests ended in a scream as he calmly picked her up and stepped inside the shower with her.

Carly pounded his chest, wailing at the top of her lungs as the icy water pummeled them. Dex held her firmly against his chest, gritting his teeth against the frigid water.

Refusing to release her, he turned a deaf ear to her pleas for mercy as the cold water soaked them. It took a full five minutes before he could feel the fight finally begin to drain out of her.

When it did, she wrapped her arms around his neck, buried her face against his neck, and sobbed in humiliation. She had done it again. Made a complete, total fool of herself in front of him.

They stood under the water until Dex was convinced that she was beginning to sober up. Stepping out of the shower, he reached for a large towel, which he wrapped around her shoulders. By now her face was a pale green, and he knew what was about to happen even before she blindly pushed him out the door and slammed it shut.

Peeling out of his wet clothes, he shook his head when he heard her long, racking heaves.

He bet it would be a while before she'd drink another gallon of anything.

When she finally emerged from the bathroom, he was waiting for her.

Glancing at him resentfully, she accepted the glass containing a mixture of tomato juice, raw egg, and Tabasco sauce he offered her, and sat down. Her first and last hangover was going to be memorable.

"You need a toothbrush?"

"I used yours."

He winced painfully.

Tipping the glass up, she downed the mixture hurriedly. Then she handed the glass back to him, pushed her wet hair out of her face, and sighed. "Well, I guess I made a perfect fool of myself."

He smiled, setting the glass on the nightstand. "Not perfect, but pretty damn close."

Typical Dex, she couldn't even make a perfect fool of herself to his way of thinking.

She glanced down, surveying her wet clothes dismally. "My suit is ruined."

Stepping closer, he drew her slowly into his arms. "I'll buy you a new one."

Carly's stomach felt as if it were tied in knots, and she wasn't sure if it was his closeness or the results of the liquor. The way he was looking at her, all warm and loving, made her want to cry.

Her arms automatically slipped around his neck, and Carly gazed into his eyes with all the love she felt. She wasn't sure what she had said or done—and she didn't care to know. She just knew that she loved him and hoped that she hadn't said something to offend him. "I'm sorry . . . I've had a really bad . . . year," she said lamely. "I'll go now."

Her knees turned to water as he lifted her to her feet and drew her closer, his mouth lowering to nuzzle her neck. "What's your hurry, tig?"

"Well . . . I . . ." She was finding it hard to think. She suddenly wasn't sure what was pounding hardest, her head or her heart.

"You can't go out in those wet clothes." His fingers casually began to unfasten the buttons on her blouse. Sighing, she parted her lips, welcoming his tongue with hers. She suspected he was going to make love to her now, and she didn't care. She welcomed his love in any form he chose to give it.

Undoing the button on her skirt, Dex worked the fabric down over her hips, allowing it to fall to the floor. Easing her out of her jacket, he tossed it to a nearby chair.

"Dex," she murmured, her fingers clinging weakly to the lapels of his terry-cloth robe. "I really don't think—"

"Then I won't either." Her blouse drifted to the floor, followed by her teddy a moment later.

Pressing warm kisses along her shoulder, his tongue teased her skin.

"Is it raining?" she asked faintly. She felt as if it were raining.

"No, it isn't raining." His mouth lowered to touch the swell of each breast, gently, leaving no doubt where it would be going next.

Lifting his head, he gazed at her, then lowered his mouth to hers again as he unsnapped her bra and let it fall to the floor. He drew back, admiring her wispy beige garter belt. "Damn, Winters, I hate to have to part with this."

She grinned. "But you'll force yourself."

He sighed, his breath coming more shaky now. "I'll force myself."

The garter belt fell away to join the other articles scattered across the floor.

Carly slowly eased his robe off his shoulders, her eyes growing warm with arousal. "Dex . . . did I ask you to make love to me?"

"What do you think?"

She groaned, burying her face in his neck in shame. "I did."

Tilting her head up, he touched his mouth to hers, slowly and deliciously. "If you hadn't, I would have asked you," he confessed. "I just wanted to make damn sure you remembered it when I did."

"Oh, Dex . . . I'll remember . . ."

Dex turned back the spread, and they stretched out on the bed side by side. For a long moment they lay in the dark, just holding each other. It had been such a long time. His fingers skimmed over her stomach, exploring her, drowning in the glorious, wonderful feel of her.

"I'm sorry I made you feel you had to compete with me, Carly."

She patted him lovingly, honestly sorry for

making his life so miserable. "It's okay. It's not important—just let me win the ball game."

He raised himself over her, love filling his eyes as he positioned himself above her. "Get real, Winters."

She raised her brows, having anticipated a delicious, slow reacquainting with him. Apparently, he thought differently. "Are we in a bit of a hurry, Matthews?"

She could feel his body trembling, and passion, for the moment, was all-consuming. They had been apart too long.

"I don't know about you, but I do feel a certain sense of urgency," he admitted in a voice suddenly thick with desire. He nibbled her ear, whispering something terribly naughty to her.

"I suppose we could talk about the game later," she conceded weakly. She brought her hands to his face and let herself drift with his kisses.

After all, there was no real hurry . . . was there?

Eight

Something wasn't right. Carly tried to break through the sleepy fog to determine what it was. What was that sound? She wasn't sure. Rolling over with her eyes closed, she pulled the covers up around her shoulders.

There it was again. It sounded like . . . a motor running.

She opened her eyes and looked right straight into a pair of unblinking green ones.

"Wha—?" She bolted straight up, wincing at the stab of pain that shot through her temples.

A large white Persian jumped off the bed, hitting the carpet with a muffled thump, and strode sedately from the room, her tail straight up, the end twitching with bad humor.

Carly frowned at the cat, then stared around the unfamiliar room. Reality slowly began to penetrate her cloudy mind. This was not her room!

Oh, Lord. What had she done now?

Her gaze moved around the room, pausing on the dark oak valet, where a familiar light gray Beau Brummel jacket was hanging.

Dex. Her heart plummeted with relief. It was Dex's bedroom. And she was naked in his bed. Her eyes quickly located her clothes, neatly folded on a nearby chair.

Closing her eyes against the wash of embarrassment, Carly covered her head with the edge of the sheet. Jeez! Now what had she done!

Memories of the night before filtered slowly back to her. She had no idea how she'd gotten to Dex's apartment or what condition she'd been in when she'd arrived. She vaguely recalled drinking a peach schnapps with Joanne—no—maybe it had been two peach schnappses. Darn, she wasn't sure!

Burying her face in her hands, she tried to still the war drums pounding in her head.

Cold shower—she remembered that—then being sick. Brushing her teeth—with whose toothbrush?

Falling back against the pillow, she heard the sound of crackling paper. Lifting her hand above the pillow, her fingers searched for the culprit. Grasping the piece of paper, she brought it to eye level and tried to focus on it:

Had to be at the office early. There's coffee and juice in the kitchen. L.Y.—Dex.

Carly crumpled the note in her hand. L.Y. Love You.

Groaning, she braced her arms across her knees and rested her head, trying to recall how big a fool she'd made of herself. She had a sinking suspicion that it was worse than she wanted to know. What had she said? Had she admitted that she was still in love with him? Please . . . no.

Climbing out of the bed, she recoiled as she saw her puffy feet. Jeez! They looked like two fat pillows! She picked up her clothes and disappeared into the bathroom, trying to keep her head from falling off her shoulders.

The cat was nowhere in sight when Carly dragged into the kitchen later. Coffee and fresh juice awaited her. Forcing herself to drink a small glass of juice, she glanced around the neat kitchen, hoping it had all been just a dream, except the part about Dex making love to her, the things he'd whispered into her ear, the places he'd touched.

Pouring a mug of coffee, she carried it with her into the living room to search for her shoes. She found them set neatly beside the door waiting for her.

"If it's a dream, the props are accurate," she muttered. "Good old tidy Dex."

After wedging the shoes into her purse, no hope of getting them back on her feet, she reached for the phone to call a cab.

Twenty minutes later she emerged from the cab in front of her apartment. Her cheeks were the color of cherry Popsicles as she crept past the doorman.

Raymond's eyes twinkled perceptively. "Good morning, Ms. Winters."

"Morning, Raymond," she muttered.

Jeez!

Carly spent the morning in her office reading reports. If anyone thought she was acting strange, they had the discretion not to mention it.

About midmorning Carly decided she could make it to the coffee bar. Rummaging through her stash of medicines, she located the aspirin. She dropped two pills into her mouth and burned her tongue in the process of trying to wash them down with hot coffee.

Carly looked up to find Dex placing his cup beneath the coffee spigot. Her face flushed a thousand shades of red as she tried to avoid looking at him. This was the moment she'd been dreading all morning. What was she supposed to say? Should she thank him for taking care of her, or curse him for . . . taking care of her?

"Hi." He lifted his brows and studied her profile. "How do you feel?"

"Like a prize fool."

"What makes you say that?" He grinned, and she felt even more foolish.

"What are you grinning about?"

"Was I grinning?"

"Like a Cheshire cat."

Winking, he dumped cream and two sugars into his coffee. "Sleep well?"

Carly wished the floor would open up and swallow her as she hurriedly busied herself dumping artificial sweetener into her cup. "Did you?"

"Like a rock." He tossed the stirrer into the wastebasket.

"You should have awakened me," she whispered. "I was nearly late for work this morning."

"Why? I was planning to cover for you."

She glanced up at him, and her stomach curled into a knot. They had made love more than once last night; that much she could remember. And it had been so incredibly wonderful.

"I left word with Mireille to wake you."

"Mireille?" Carly frowned. It had been so easy to forget about Mireille. "I thought she was in the hospital."

"Naw, she's out now. You sure she didn't wake you? She's usually dependable."

"No . . . your cat woke me."

"Yeah." he smiled. "As I said, Mireille's pretty dependable."

He turned and casually sauntered down the hall.

Carly was lifting her cup to her mouth when her hand suddenly froze in midair.

Mireille?

Mireille!

She whirled. "Mireille is a cat?"

Chuckling, Dex ducked into his office and closed the door behind him.

Carly marched back to her office and slammed the door, wincing as the noise set off a chain of explosions in her pulsating brain.

He'd had her half out of her mind with jealousy over a cat! He'd wanted to buy a balloon bouquet for a cat!

Sinking into her chair, she buried her face in her lap. Why did she let him get to her this way? Because she loved him. . . . She was a dolt, but she loved him.

After a sigh she leaned back in her chair and started to giggle. Before long she was laughing out loud. Mireille wasn't a piece of French toast, Mireille was a cat! A cat!

A knock sounded at the door and Carly bolted upright, wiping tears of relief from her eyes.

"Yes?"

Martin poked his head around the door. "Got a minute?"

"Sure. Come in, Martin."

Martin stepped in and seated himself in the chair in front of her desk. "How would you like a pleasant surprise?"

"You've canceled the ball game?"

He looked genuinely taken aback. "Goodness, no. Why would you say that?"

"Wishful thinking."

"No, the game is still on." Martin leaned back, relaxing. "What I wanted to discuss with you has to do with the reorganization process: Dex wants to move a couple of people from marketing to research."

"Really? Does he have anyone in particular in mind?"

"Jack Lathier to begin."

"Jack. From marketing? Why?"

"Dex feels he'll be more valuable in research."

Carly sat up straighter. "You're kidding." Rumor had it that Jack had played with a farm team in Chicago before joining Montrose.

"The three of us had a meeting this morning, and Jack had no objections to making the move. If you'd want him—"

"Want him! Of course I want him!" If the gossip was credible, Jack would be a godsend for her ball team! She'd already told Pat Brown that he'd be pitching in Saturday's game, but that wouldn't be necessary now.

Carly tried to recall what they had said about Jack—something about his choosing to leave baseball because he didn't want to be on the road, away from his wife and twin sons?

"Actually, Jack's degree is in business. Though he found advertising and marketing interesting, he told me he prefers working with figures and research, and he might enjoy the challenge of being on the bottom floor of a project," Martin said.

"Makes sense to me. When can I have him?"

"Dex would like to make the move effective immediately."

Carly couldn't believe her luck, but she wasn't about to question it.

"Great. Then can I consider Jack mine? Today?"

"Looks that way."

Hot dog! She was back in the ball game!

"Dex wants to move Sharon Miller sometime in the near future, so be advised."

"Martin"—Carly extended her hand gratefully—"I'm advised—and you've just saved my life."

Martin laughed. "Not me. Thank Dex."

"Of course," Carly corrected herself. "As always, thank Dex."

After Martin left, Carly picked up the phone and punched Jack's extension number. After officially welcoming him to research, Carly drafted him into the ball practice scheduled for that afternoon. He said he'd be there, and Carly hung up a happy woman.

As she drove to the ball field that afternoon, she wondered why Dex hadn't recruited Jack for marketing's team. He would be aware of the man's background from his personnel files. He could have easily delayed the departmental transfer until after the game, if he'd wanted. But he hadn't. Why?

Oh, Lord. Jack must not be any good. That's it. Dex could have had Jack, but he didn't want him. Carly beat her fist on the steering wheel. Jeez! How could she have been so gullible!

Most of the team was already there when Carly wheeled into the parking lot. She could see her new employee on the mound, warming up. Keeping an eye on him, she balanced against her bumper, strapping on her protection equipment.

Zzzzzzzzzipp!

Zzzzzzzzzipp!

Two fast balls, straight over home plate!

Zzzzzzzzzzzipp!.

Zzzzzzzzzzzzzzzzzipppp!

A gorgeous curve!

Picking up the sack of bats, Carly trotted to the bench and deposited the gear. For a moment she just stood and watched her newfound fortune. Jack was good! He was throwing blue smoke! He even looked like a ball player with his worn cleats, old sweatshirt, and rumpled sweat pants.

The rest of her team members stood in awe, their mouths hanging open as he rocked back and fired ball after ball straight over home plate.

Carly looked up to see Dex sitting in the empty bleachers, watching.

Spotting her, he waved, and she lifted her hand to wave back. He was still dressed in his suit and tie, so she assumed he had just left the office.

Carly found it hard to concentrate when the practice finally got under way. Her thoughts were on the man she'd spent the previous night with.

Concentrate, Carly, she told herself. She had to win this ball game.

She wasn't sure when winning the ball game had become so important to her. Maybe deep in the back of her mind, she harbored the knowledge that if she could win—fair and square—she would have laid her fears of inadequacy to rest.

Silly reasoning, but if she could beat Dex—just once—at anything—she knew she had a shot at putting their relationship back together again. She guessed what it all boiled down to was the fact that she was tired of making a fool of herself in front of Dex. She had to stop that if she had any hopes of getting him back. Starting right now, he wasn't going to see anything but the cosmopolitan side of Carly Winters.

Practice went smoothly that afternoon. The team looked good with no opposing team to call attention to the errors.

The eighth batter foul-tipped the ball, and Carly ripped off her mask and made a beeline to catch it. She took her eye off the ball for only one second, while checking to see if Dex was watching the play. At that instant she ran straight into the backstop.

Her body ricocheted off the fence like a rubber mallet.

Still quivering, she lay on her back, trying to regain her senses.

The ball came down and plopped dead at her feet.

From the upper bleachers she heard a lone person clapping.

Shooting a dirty look in Dex's direction, she got up, dusted the dirt off her pants, then put her mask on again.

So much for cosmoplitan.

After practice Carly drew Jack aside to tell him how much she appreciated his participation.

"You're going to help us a lot," she said. "You may have noticed hardly anyone knows what he's doing."

Jack laughed. "I noticed. But you're not bad behind the plate. I'll try to watch the fast ball."

He'd burned a fast ball across the plate and had knocked Carly off her feet twice.

Carly laughed. "I'll be prepared next time."

Jack got a drink from the water fountain, then began stowing his gear in his satchel. Carly fell into step beside him as they walked toward the parking lot.

"I'm glad you'll be joining research, us. We can use a man with your experience."

"I'm looking forward to the challenge—"

"Hey, Lathier, going for pizza and a beer with us?" One of the other players leaned on the open door of his car, motioning for Jack to join him.

"No can do. Jill has a PTA meeting tonight, and I have to watch the kids."

"Carly."

Carly turned to find Hayden standing at the fence, waving to her. She quickly squelched the stab of disappointment she felt when she saw him. She'd been anticipating another evening with Dex.

Walking to the fence, she spotted Dex standing next to his car talking with two men from research. She realized then that she had been planning to ask Dex to go for pizza.

"Hayden, what an unexpected surprise." Carly hooked her fingers into the fence and rested against it.

"Since you keep canceling out on me, I thought I'd stop by and see how you're doing."

"Hey, Carly, let's go!" someone shouted.

"Be there in a minute," Carly called back.

"Do you have plans?" Hayden asked.

"Not really. The team's going to Bonner's for pizza. Want to come?"

"Would you mind?"

"Mind?" She laughed. "Of course I wouldn't mind, Hayden." She felt so guilty that she reached out and touched his hand gently. "I'm sorry. I have neglected you lately, haven't I?"

Hayden smiled weakly. "I know you've been busy."

Not that busy, Carly conceded silently. After last night she knew that she could no longer continue seeing Hayden. She wasn't sure where she and Dex were heading, but she knew she had absolutely no future with Hayden.

"I think if we're going to date we really should go out with each other occasionally," Hayden said in a confiding tone.

"Give me a minute to get out of this gear, then you can follow me to Bonner's in your car," she said.

Somehow, she'd find a way to tell him.

*   *   *

Twenty minutes later Hayden parked beside her car in the parking lot of the local pub that had become an after-practice hangout for the team. Everyone was there, including Dex, when they arrived.

Taking a deep breath, Carly made her way through the crowded room, aware that she was tired of trying to keep a stiff upper lip when she was around Dex. They had to talk eventually. What had happened last night couldn't be ignored forever.

As they approached the table, Dex stood up to discard his jacket. He smiled at her, more charmingly than Carly thought necessary, as he casually rolled up his shirt-sleeves.

Carly purposely avoided meeting his eyes. "Save me a place," she murmured to Hayden. "I want to wash up."

"Sure, go ahead. I'll order. Pepperoni and onions?"

"Better make it a hamburger," Dex corrected her absently.

Hayden glanced at him. "Hamburger?"

Dex nodded. "It's blander. Her stomach has been a little out of whack today, and onions give her the hiccups."

"Oh?" Hayden looked at Carly. "I didn't know onions gave you hiccups."

"Not all the time." Her eyes met Dex's resentfully.

"Pepperoni and onions sounds great."

Dex smiled, shrugging lazily. "It's your stomach."

When Carly returned from the bathroom, Hayden was seated next to Greta. The only empty chair left was next to Dex.

The noise level was high. Carly could hardly hear herself think as she sat down. Her leg bumped Dex's, and he glanced at her.

She quickly averted her gaze, aware that he was watching her with a knowing smile on his lips.

"Something funny?" she countered beneath her breath.

"Not that I know of."

"I've ordered," Hayden called to her as he slid a mug of beer in front of her.

Carly glanced at the beer, then involuntarily up at Dex. A grin crinkled the corners of his eyes. "You're not really going to drink that."

"I might."

But she left the beer alone as she pretended to listen to the long, involved story one of the players was telling. She managed to laugh at the appropriate places, though her heart wasn't in it. Her head hurt, and she wished she could go home and have a good, long cry.

Here she was, sitting beside the man who had made love to her last night, and she couldn't touch him, brush his hand, lean over and whisper into his ear, or anything. She had to pretend that he meant nothing more to her than any other man sitting at the table.

Greta and David got up to dance when a slow, romantic ballad came on the jukebox.

Carly's headache began to pound harder when Hayden looked at her questioningly. "Want to dance?"

"Oh, Hayden, I'm so dirty—"

Hayden stood up and held out his hand. "So is everyone else."

She didn't really want to dance, not with Hayden. But a moment later she allowed herself to be led onto the dance floor.

Hayden held her at the proper distance—not too close, not too loose. Moving around the small floor, Carly closed her eyes, determined not to look Dex's way.

Her feet moved mechanically through the steps as Willie Nelson sang about blue eyes crying in the rain. Carly knew exactly how he felt.

The song went on and on. Carly finally made her mind a complete blank. Hayden had never claimed to be a dancer, so she wasn't surprised that he didn't feel the music. It reminded her of how she'd danced with her brothers when she was younger, letting them practice steps with her before the night of the senior dance.

Dancing had always come easy to her, while Hayden had once confessed that he was a graduate of Arthur Murray's. Carly could tell he still counted rhythm to himself.

"You're being a blockhead," Carly murmured absently to herself. "You're in a nasty mood, and you're taking it out on poor Hayden."

Hayden drew back. "Pardon?"

She smiled. "Nice song."

"Yeah." He drew her closer as her gaze involuntarily drifted to Dex. When she realized that Dex was watching her, she quickly shut her eyes again. Flashes of last night—lying in his arms—crowded her mind, taunting her, teasing her.

"Hayden?"

"Yes."

She knew it was the poor timing: Hayden deserved to be let down easily, but her conscience was killing her. "I can't see you anymore."

Hayden's steps faltered momentarily, then he discreetly recovered. They danced in silence for a moment.

"I suppose I should ask why," he finally said.

"Because I'm still in love with Dex," she said quietly.

She felt him tense, but only for an instant. "I think I had just about figured that out."

"Not that he feels the same about me—I mean, I know he cares about me, but we still have a lot of differences."

"But you would like to be free to explore those differences?"

"No." She shook her head. That sounded too presumptuous. After all, she had no idea what Dex was thinking. "I just want to be honest with you."

As the song died away, Hayden squeezed her waist reassuringly. Carly knew that her declaration had come as no surprise, yet she was relieved to see that he was going to accept it.

The pizza arrived as they returned to the table. The next few minutes were chaotic as the various orders were sorted out and the waitress tried to determine who had ordered what.

Carly's stomach revolted when the spicy pepperoni and onion hit bottom, but after managing to get through one slice, she felt better and reached for a second.

"Better eat the hamburger," Dex warned next to her. "You'll be sick."

"I will not." Carly signaled the waitress and ordered a 7-Up.

Finally, only a few slices remained from the three giant supers, one with anchovies and two without, and the lone pepperoni and onion. The group sat back to let the meal settle.

Someone got up and pumped another quarter into the jukebox and an old favorite of Carly's began playing. Involuntarily, her eyes drifted to Dex's.

A moment later he casually stood, holding out his hand to her. Carly didn't try to pretend she wasn't interested this time. She stood up and accepted his hand, and he led her to the dance floor.

"Relax. I don't bite," he murmured as she came into his arms.

"Then what is that strange brown thing I found on my neck this morning?"

He grinned, pulling her to him. "Just dance."

Laying her head on his shoulder, she relaxed, moving in time to the music with him. They fit together like lock and key.

"Did you transfer Jack into research just so I would have a pitcher?"

"Not me."

"Dex, seriously." Carly had been thinking about the move. It seemed to have come at an awfully convenient time.

"I transferred Jack into research because that's where I think he needs to be—and I don't intend to get into another argument over it."

"I don't either, but if you did transfer him to give me a pitcher in place of Greta, I'll be mad."

"What's new?"

"Because I plan to beat you fair and square."

"Why do I have the feeling that this ball game has become some personal vendetta that you're hell-bent on settling between us?"

"It isn't—I just planned to win Saturday, that's all."

They danced for a moment, holding each other almost indecently close. Carly felt warm and liquid in his arms, and she didn't care who was watching. They were good together. They always had been.

"By the way, it was mean of you to make me think Mireille was your girlfriend," she accused.

"When did I say that Mireille was my girlfriend?" His breath was warm against her ear, and her stomach reacted erratically.

"Dex, don't."

"That's not what you said last night."

"And about last night . . ."

His hold tightened as he guided her to the far side of the floor, away from the table where the others sat. When they reached the shadows, his mouth lowered to close over hers. Their feet paused as Carly's arms slipped around his neck, and they kissed. Balancing on her toes, Carly deepened the kiss, hungrily.

"About last night," he whispered into her mouth, "it was pretty damn wonderful." His words sent shivers down her spine, making it impossible to make her thoughts rational.

"You know, I have the feeling that the only reason you came back was to make me admit that I regret breaking our engagement." The accusation was out before Carly could stop it.

"You were always good with hunches."

Pulling back, she looked at him. "You admit it?"

"Sure."

"Was that what last night was all about? You, achieving your goal?"

"You appeared at *my* door last night. Remember?"

She loosened his hold, angry that she had played right into his hands.

Their feet automatically began moving again. "Did . . . did I admit that I was sorry?" she asked.

Carly remembered that there had been a passionate exchange of words last night, she just wasn't sure who had admitted what.

"I think I'll let you stew about that for a while."

"Why, you—"

Calmly drawing her back to him, Dex held her firmly as she continued to try to squirm out of his grasp.

"Let me go. You've had your fun."

"No I haven't. Believe me, this past year has been anything but fun."

"Well, it hasn't been a barrel of laughs for me either. I made a mistake. Okay? I was wrong. I was stupid for breaking our engagement. You were right, and, as usual, I was wrong. Happy now?"

"No. It doesn't make me happy."

Carly wheeled and walked off, leaving him standing alone on the dance floor.

Dex watched her go, wondering why her admission hadn't made him feel as good as he'd thought it would. So, maybe he had dreamed of this moment for fifty-two long weeks: hearing her admit that she had been wrong.

On his way back to the table, he knew that it was now time for phase two.

Nine

When she opened her eyes on Saturday the sky was a flawless blue. The inevitable could not be avoided. Carly seriously thought about praying for some rain clouds to soak them by afternoon, but with her luck the game would be held anyway. And the prospect of slogging around knee-deep in mud and *still* getting whipped was even worse than losing the game on a sunny day.

She rolled to her side and squinted at the clock. In ninety minutes she would be expected at the park, prepared to meet her fate.

After struggling out of bed, a couple of minutes later she was standing under the shower, still hoping for a miracle.

Leaning against the tile wall, she closed her eyes and let the water wash over her. Memories of Dex filled her, dancing with him, making love with him, *being* in love with him, and not knowing what to do now. Dex—what was she going to do about Dex? It had hurt when he'd told her he'd returned only to hear her say that she had made a mistake. It seemed infantile, juvenile, and completely out of character for him. He wasn't prone to being childish, was he? In the past he had always seemed so philosophical about life's vagaries.

Gritting her teeth, she flipped the water temperature to cold, determined to abolish his memory. Maybe it was time for her to think seriously about changing jobs. When she had broken their engagement a year ago, she'd strongly considered it. She'd been with Montrose a good part of her adult life. Maybe it was time to make a change. Now that Dex was back, she couldn't continue working with him every day, loving him the way she did. She still had her pride, though it was coming a bit unraveled.

On Monday she would call a good job placement service and set the wheels in motion. Of course, Dex would think she was leaving because of the ball game she was sure to lose, but she'd know the real reason: she was running away from him again.

Thirty minutes later, Carly stowed her gear in the trunk and got into the Camaro.

When she was just two blocks from the park, traffic slowed to a crawl. By the time she inched her way onto the lot and seized the last available parking spot, her worst fears were realized. Everyone and his uncle had come to witness the slaughter. The bleachers were packed.

Unlocking the trunk of her car, she quickly surveyed the manicured lawn. Today it was liberally decorated with blankets, children, balloons, and various games for the kids. A clown was busy blowing up balloons and twisting them into animal shapes for the little ones. Members of a band occupied the gazebo, setting up speakers and other equipment. Long rows of tables stretched along one length of the park, and catering trucks from a local barbecue were lining the curb.

After dragging out her duffel bag, Carly slammed the trunk lid shut, then walked slowly toward the ball diamond. Members of the research team were already warming up on the field.

She quickly scanned the crowd, locating Dex with his team surrounding him at the back of the field.

Dex hadn't said much about his team, and she knew little about their ability except for the one time the two teams had practiced together. The marketing team had been terrific then, so it would be fair to assume that by now they were awesome.

Dumping her bag onto the bench, she walked to home plate and surveyed center field apprehensively. It was deep—today the four hundred feet looked more like four hundred miles. Even with Jack's expertise there was no way her team could make a decent showing. Unless Jack pitched a no-hitter, which she admitted would be tough.

An air of festivity reigned as the band struck up a spirited tune. Carly glanced up into the bleachers and saw Martin and his wife trying to seat their five grandchildren.

The large American flag popped feistily in the strong southerly breeze as Carly began to unload the balls and bats and line them up near the backstop.

A few minutes before the game was to begin, the crowd came to their feet to sing the national anthem.

Applause and whistles broke out as Carly and Dex walked to the mound, each with a wad of bubble gum stuck against their inner jaw. Carly purposefully avoided meeting Dex's eyes as the umpire began to outline the rules and the foul lines. He was probably afraid that she was still upset about the night before. And rightly so.

She'd drafted Mort from layout to be umpire. "If the ball rolls into the dugout, ball's dead; runner advances one base. There'll be no mouthing, and no bat throwing. Anyone wants to complain, it has to be through the coach. It's easier to throw one person out of the game than the whole bench. Understood?"

Carly and Dex nodded.

"Okay." Mort flipped a coin to see who would bat first.

"Heads," Carly said.

The coin landed on the back of Mort's hand, and Carly rose on tiptoe to view the results.

"Tails." Damn. Now marketing would be considered the home team.

"Tough break." Dex grinned.

She forced herself to shake his hand as a gesture of good sportsmanship.

When Dex held on a little longer than necessary, she removed her hand from his.

"Still mad at me?"

When she turned around and walked away without answering, Dex felt he could safely assume that she was.

A moment later Carly was in full gear, squatting behind home plate. She braced herself, waiting for Jack's first pitch.

Dex was finding it hard to concentrate on the game . . . and keep his eyes off Carly's bottom as he took a seat on the opposing bench. Her white shorts and snug Montrose T-shirt just plain unnerved him. The combination set off a chain reaction inside him that he knew was going to prove embarrassing if he didn't get his mind on the game. Reaching for his clipboard, he whistled for Mel Logan to take the plate just as he heard the umpire call, "Play ball!"

The first ball burned across the plate. The crowd waited for the umpire to make the call.

After thinking about it for a moment, Mort bent halfway down on his knee, raised his right hand, and said, "Stttrrrrike!"

Bounding to her feet, Carly gave Jack a thumbs-up sign before returning the ball.

Seconds later the ball came whizzing toward home plate again, broke slightly to the right, and barreled across the base.

Mel took a wild swing, nearly losing his balance as he went after the wild pitch.

Zzzzaaappp!

The ball landed firmly in Carly's glove, and Mort gyrated to his right, went halfway down to his knee, and shouted, "Sttrrrike two!"

The crowd cheered as a clown suddenly bounded out onto the field and began cheerleading, directing the crowd in a "wave," which brought hoots of laughter.

The third pitch was a ball, and the crowd hooted and jeered. Jack was off to a good start, but Carly's hands were burning like fire from the strength of his pitches.

Mel hit a short hop to second and was promptly thrown out at first a few moments later.

The second batter strutted to the plate. She gripped the bat tightly, keeping her eye on the ball as it came hurling toward her. Shutting her eyes, she swung, sending a grounder down to first base. The ball was easily fielded, and Joe Madison stepped onto the bag for the second out.

The third batter had a solid hit to center field. Dana started running for the ball as Carly jumped up, flung off her mask, and yelled.

The men on both teams stopped dead in their tracks to watch Dana run.

The ball dropped two inches away from Dana, but she was on it like a chicken on a kernel of corn. She made the throw back to first, and the ball arrived just a hair ahead of the runner.

Carly jumped up and down, screaming, "Way to go! Way to go!"

Third out, no score.

Running back to the dugout, Carly passed by Dex. "In your face!" she taunted. She realized she wasn't being nice, but neither was Dex.

Ignoring her, Dex calmly picked up his glove and walked to third base.

Research was at bat approximately four and a half minutes. No one got a hit; no one even came close.

Once again Carly squatted behind home plate, praying that Jack would fan the next three batters.

The first hit a pop fly to the infield. The shortstop bobbled the ball and finally lobbed a limp toss to first base, but the runner was already on the way to second.

The first and second basemen caught the runner in a run-down situation. In the end he panicked and darted outside the base line. He was called out, and Carly nearly fainted with relief.

Squatting behind the plate again, Carly realized that her knees were already killing her and she still had eight more innings to go.

"Okay, guys," she yelled. "One more!"

Her heart sank as she saw Dex walking to the plate. When he reached it, he stopped and tapped the bat against his cleats. Stretching the gum out on his tongue, he formed a bubble, then blew it as he wedged the bat between his thighs and rubbed rosin on his hands.

"Will you just get up there and bat?" Carly growled when he had piddled around for over two minutes.

Dex glanced at the umpire. "I thought you said there's not supposed to be any mouthing."

"Will you just get up there and bat!" Carly snapped. Her nerves were humming like a telephone wire.

"Batter up!" The ump called.

Dex stepped into the batter's box. Lifting the bat to his shoulder, he tightened his grip.

Carly tensed, waiting for the pitch. This was one out she was going to enjoy.

The ball zipped over the plate.

Ball one.

Stepping out of the box, Dex tapped the dirt off his cleats with the bat, straightened his hat, his crotch, then spit.

Carly watched with disgust, wondering if he thought he imagined he was a professional player, earning a million dollars a year.

Moving back into the box, Dex noticed Carly eyeing him. "You got a problem, Winters?"

"Yeah, you."

"You're still hacked about last night, aren't you?"

"How did you guess?"

Dex grinned, gripping the bat tighter as he resumed his batting stance.

"I know you, baby."

Her cheeks flamed hotly as she glanced at the umpire. "I thought you said no mouthing."

"Play ball!" the ump ordered.

Dex straightened and lifted the bat to his shoulder. Irritated, Carly raised her glove as a target.

Suddenly his hand shot up, calling a time-out. A moment later he stepped out of the box again.

Carly fell onto her back melodramatically.

When Jack was finally allowed to deliver the second pitch, it was a nice fast ball.

Strike one.

Not bad, Carly thought. She would have bet her last Twinkie that marketing would have been three runs ahead by now, but they weren't.

She viewed her team and suddenly realized that with all the changes Dex had been making lately, both teams were fairly evenly matched.

The third ball curved inside at the last minute, and Carly dove for it, sliding facefirst into the dirt.

Dex watched as she wallowed at his feet, swearing like a sailor as she tried to retrieve the elusive ball.

Dex glanced at the umpire. "Isn't there a rule against swearing?"

Carly whacked him across the shins with her glove, and he jumped defensively but didn't comment again.

The third ball cracked solidly against Dex's bat and went soaring deep into center field.

Carly leapt to her feet, jerked off her face mask, and threw it in the dirt as the ball sailed toward the fence.

She was reminded of the Keystone Cops as all three research outfielders went running toward the ball at the same time.

Carly watched in horror as the left fielder and center fielder hit head-on, flipping both of them straight up in the air.

The right fielder scrambled madly over the pile of limp bodies in a frenzied attempt to make the catch. The ball dropped and bounced twenty feet as she chased it down the outfield.

Once she had the ball in hand, she drew back and threw it. It landed six feet in front of her. She scurried to retrieve it, snatched it up, and heaved it another six feet. In three throws she managed to get the ball out of the outfield to the second baseman.

By now everyone in the stands was on their feet, yelling. Dex was rounding third base and heading for home, running like a bat out of hell.

Carly parked herself in front of home plate and screamed for the ball. "Home it! Send it home!"

Her heart hammered wildly as she watched Dex barreling down the homestretch toward her. If he collided with her, she'd be nothing but a grease spot on the mound. But he wouldn't hit her; he was too much of a gentleman to do that.

She thumped her glove, raising it higher and shouting, "Throw the ball—"

Dex streaked across the plate as the ball hit Carly's glove and her feet flew out from beneath her. She went down with Dex in an explosion of oaths and flailing limbs.

Cheers and jeers filled the air as the two wallowed in the dirt, trying to disengage themselves.

"Get off me!"

"Dammit, Carly, why didn't you get out of my way!"

"Because I'm the catcher!"

"Touch base, touch base!" one of the people from marketing was shouting at Dex.

Spying an escape hole, Dex crawled beneath Carly and slapped his hand on the plate.

The ump dipped smoothly, scissoring his hands back and forth. "Saaafe!"

The crowd roared.

Bounding to her feet, Carly went nose to nose with Mort. "Safe? Are you crazy, Mort? I had the ball in my glove! He's out!"

Mort viewed her empty glove calmly. "You don't have the ball now."

Carly glanced down, realizing that she must have dropped the ball in the scuffle.

Mort repeated, "Safe."

Carly still wasn't convinced. "Isn't there some rule about interfering with the catcher?" she demanded.

The ump motioned to the marketing team. "Batter up!"

Glaring at him, Carly put her mask on again, vowing to win now if it killed her.

Dex dusted off the seat of his pants as he calmly ambled back to the bench.

The numbers on the scoreboard rolled over. Home team one. Visitors zero.

Jim the next batter fouled the first pitch. Dex appeared none too happy about the situation. When he called time, Carly shook her head wordlessly, anticipating another scratching, tapping, spitting session.

Stepping back into the box a moment later, Jim hefted the bat to his shoulder, waiting for the pitch.

"Shoe's untied."

Jim glanced down at her. "What?"

The ball zipped over the plate.

"Strrriiiike!"

Jim swore and tightened his grip on the bat. Concentrating, he waited for the second ball.

"Shoe's untied."

He whirled. "What?"

Zip.

"Strrriiiike twooo!"

Emerging from the bench, Dex walked to the plate, calling time.

"What's the problem?" he asked as he drew Jim aside.

Jim jerked his head toward Carly. "She's heckling me."

Carly's eyes widened innocently. "I am not!"

"Cut it out, Carly," Dex warned. His tone clearly implied *or else.*

"I'm not doing anything."

"See that you keep it that way."

She watched as Dex turned and walked back to the bench.

"Okay, Jack, lay it in here." She thumped her glove expectantly.

Jim stepped back to the box and resumed his stance. He waited, keeping an eye on the ball.

Jack drew back and threw.

"Fly's open."

Jim whirled to confront her this time. "What?"

Zip.

"Strriiike, a three!"

"Aw." Carly smiled. "Tough luck, Jim." She stood up and threw the ball back to Jack as Jim left the plate red-faced, grumbling his way back to the bench to the hoots and calls of the spectators.

"Okay!" Carly yelled exuberantly. "Two down, one to go!"

The third batter stepped to the box and tapped the plate with his bat. He peered at Jack beneath bushy brows, shifting a wad of tobacco to his right jaw.

"Heads up, team. This one's a killer!"

A pop fly to left field enabled the runner to get to first.

Carly relaxed for a moment. Dex was on deck again, calmly swinging his bat. The play of muscles in his arms sent goose bumps up her spine.

For a moment she forgot all about the ball game.

For a moment all she could think of was how she would like to be alone somewhere with him right now—completely alone.

Dex slipped the weight off his bat and strolled to the plate as Jack walked the batter.

"Ooohhhh, got th' captain here," Carly mocked. "Big cheese comin' up to bat. Heads up, guys."

Dex settled into his batter's stance, watching as Jack drew back, then delivered the ball.

"Cute buns," she said.

"Thanks."

Carly winced at the sound of the ear-splitting crack. The ball went up, soaring through the air and over the fence like a bullet.

The crowd roared as Dex trotted around the bases, exchanging high-fives, high-sixes, and every other kind of high with everyone he passed.

Dropping to the ground, Carly buried her head in her lap and waited until he was through hot-dogging.

The next hour was a blur to Carly. The batters came and went. Balls, strikes, fouls, foul-tips, runners advancing, players being thrown out—it all began to look the same to her.

By the time Carly's team came to bat in the bottom of the eighth, its spirit was sinking fast. By now she wouldn't even look at Dex.

"This is too close to call," one of her team-mates said.

"I'm surprised we're still in the game."

"Me too. If someone hadn't bobbled the last three balls—"

"You think you can do any better, Winters? I didn't want to play this game—"

Carly unstrapped her gear, eyeing the complainers sourly. "Come on, you guys. Stop griping and just do the best you can." She glanced at Jack, who by now appeared to be in real pain. "You going to be able to make it?"

Jack shook his head apologetically. "I think you'd better warm up Pat. I think I've had it."

Carly nodded, all hope of winning vanished. Without Jack, she didn't have a prayer.

She paused. Suddenly she realized what she'd been thinking.

Carly, listen to you! Why is it you have to beat Dex? It's a team effort—win or lose. Why couldn't she see this game for what it really was? It was just a simple softball game, not a life-threatening contest of will between her and the man she loved. She realized Dex was right. She was the one making everything difficult—not him.

When Carly walked to the plate five minutes later, the bases were loaded. She didn't know how they had gotten that way. She had been so troubled by her own thoughts, she hadn't been watching.

Had she really given up the most important

thing in her life just because of her chronic need to win?

She swung at the first ball.

"Stttrrriiike one!"

She let the second one go without a glance.

She knew she'd given up Dex for some stupid reason. She was a victim of her own overblown ego. She felt like an idiot.

"Stttrrriiike two!"

Gripping the handle of the bat, she tried to concentrate. She could feel sweat trickling down the sides of her face now. *No, you couldn't have been so foolish*, she kept telling herself. She couldn't have— But she had . . .

The pitch came inside and she stepped into it, hitting the ball into the outfield.

"Run!" The crowd came to their feet expectantly as Carly turned, her eyes searching for Dex, who was standing near the third base line, watching her. His brows rose in question when he saw her looking at him.

Had she done that? Had she risked losing the only man she'd ever love for such a shallow reason?

"Run!" Jill bounced up and down, shouting.

The ball bounced in front of the outfielder who fell to his knees, grappling for it.

Snapping out of her daze, Carly bolted for first, arriving just as the ball whizzed straight over the first baseman's mitt. The runners on second and third went racing for home.

"Second, second!" someone shouted.

After dashing to second, Carly's foot touched base a split second before the ball arrived.

"All right!" Random applause broke out as Carly called a time-out to tie her shoe.

Visitors, 2. Home team, 4.

Edsel Goodman walked to the batter's box.

Ordinarily, the sight of the wiry little accountant with horn-rimmed glasses would strike terror into the heart of Carly. Edsel was the worst player on the team, and hadn't hit the ball once— at practice or otherwise.

But Carly suddenly found herself encouraging Edsel, calling to him hopefully, "Come on Edsel, you can do it."

Edsel swung at the first wild pitch, sending the ball flying through the air. Up, up, up it went, soaring toward the left-field fence.

Bedlam broke out as Carly raced to third. Elated, she felt Dex reach out and swat her supportively on her backside as she headed for home. Her heart was pounding as hard as her feet as she glanced back and shot him a grin.

He winked at her, and her heart sang!

The ball had rolled to the far corner of left field, and Winny Ellison was still chasing it.

Edsel roared around first, then second, then third, where the base coach waved him on.

Streaking across home plate, Carly shoved one fist into the air in jubilation, turning to watch Edsel round third, pumping his legs as fast as they could carry him.

"Come on, Edsel! You can do it!" Carly shouted, jumping up and down.

Edsel's face was a mask of abject concentration as his feet thundered toward home plate.

The ball came sailing through the air, and the crowd came to its feet, urging Edsel to victory.

Diving for the plate, Edsel knocked the ball out of Phil Watson's hand and slid between his legs as his fingers touched base.

"Saaafe!"

Springing to his feet, Edsel let out a yell and pounded his chest victoriously as the score board rolled over: Visitors, 5, Home 4. It was a day that would be forever etched in Edsel's memory. When the inning was over, it had been a glorious one. The team was basking in its victory as it took the field for the last time.

Walking to the scorekeeper, Carly called the changes to him. Pat Brown was going in for Jack Lathier, and Jenny Witmer would be replacing Harry Grantham in left field.

Top of the ninth, Pat took the mound and threw a few pitches to loosen his arm.

Carly was squatted behind the plate, adjusting her face mask. She no longer cared if marketing pulled ahead. She had just witnessed a miracle and she would never again believe that something wonderful couldn't happen if a person really tried.

All she wanted now was time alone with Dex to tell him she was sorry, that she had been so terribly wrong, that nothing was worth the agony she had put them both through this past year.

She could change. She would have to change her way of thinking, but it was a needed change, one she knew she not only wanted to make, but was now capable of making.

And if Dex didn't remind her, she would remind him that they weren't competing against each other: it was the two of them against the world.

A nice combination. One she could grow old with.

Relieved to finally have the matter laid to rest, she thumped her glove, just hoping that Dex would see it the same way.

Ten

Final score: Visitors, 5, Home team, 4. Carly could hardly believe it, but marketing hadn't been able to hit the broad side of a barn in the ninth. Research had won. *Research* had won the darn game!

Caught up in a barrage of enthusiastic back-slapping, Carly scanned the field, searching for Dex, but he was nowhere to be seen.

"Phil, where's Dex?" she called above all the rowdy pandemonium.

Someone was pouring a bottle of orange soda pop over Joe Madison's head as he called something back to her that sounded like "Haven't seen him."

Carly pushed her way through the milling mass, trying to locate the familiar set of blue eyes. But Dex was gone.

She still hadn't found him an hour later as she loaded the equipment into the trunk of her car and prepared to leave the ball field. Frustrated, she perched on the bumper and removed her cleats, aching to find him. She had so much to tell him, so much apologizing to do. For the first time in a long time, she knew exactly what she wanted: Dex Matthews.

Driving by his apartment, she saw that his car wasn't there and all the windows were dark.

Did he leave the ball park with Greta? Carly tried to remember if she had seen Greta in the past hour. She couldn't recall.

Finally, around seven, she drove home, completely baffled by his disappearance.

After running a tub of cool water, she stripped off her clothes and examined her battered body in the mirror. She was suddenly aware of muscles that she hadn't known existed. Both her knees and an elbow were skinned, and a big black bruise was developing on her right hip and left thigh.

Burying her face in her hands, she began to sob. She was tired, filthy dirty, and so lonely she thought she would die.

After a good, lengthy cry, she blew her nose, then stepped into the bathtub for a long soak.

Dex, I need you so bad. Where are you?

It was close to midnight when Carly's Camaro pulled into the ball park again. She had spent the last five hours calling Dex's apartment and making the rounds of every restaurant and pub he frequented and had still come up empty-handed. He had simply disappeared from the face of the earth.

She thought by coming to the park she would be closer to him. Silly really, but she couldn't bear to return home.

She parked next to a white Regal on the moonlight-filled lot. She was crying again, and she hated that. Walking toward the ball field, she dragged a Butterfinger out of the pocket of her Windbreaker and opened it. This week's diet was shot, and it wasn't even Monday yet.

Seating herself on the empty bleachers, her eyes scanned the equally empty field, recalling the game. Martin had been elated with research's victory. He complimented Carly on the win and promised the two teams that there would be another game next year.

Well, she doubted that she would be around for it. She took a bite of candy and sniffled. If Dex ever showed up again, she was going to ask him to forgive her, then ask him to marry her, and if he refused, then she was going to look for a new job—with the precondition that she would never again captain a baseball team.

Finishing off the Butterfinger, she fished another one out of her pocket, wondering if anyone had ever died from an overdose of chocolate and peanut butter in a deserted ball park. She could be a first. All she needed was a chocolate malt to wash down the peanut butter, and she'd know that she had truly hit bottom. When she stepped on her new talking scale tomorrow morning and the voice said "One at a time, please," it would be her own fault.

The headlights of a vehicle pulling into the parking lot washed over her. Her jaws bulging with chocolate, Carly went limp with relief when she recognized Dex's Corvette.

She could hear Eddie Pantuse saying good night as he got out of the Corvette and walked to his car. He was still wearing his ball shirt, so the mystery was solved. Dex had been with Eddie all evening.

The Regal pulled out. Carly watched to see if Dex even noticed her car sitting on the lot.

The Corvette idled for a moment, then slowly began to edge toward the ball field. A minute or two later the car pulled up beside the fence next to the bleachers and stopped.

"Is that you, tig?"

"You're not supposed to drive on the grass," Carly said.

Switching off the engine, Dex got out of the car. He swung over the fence, quickly scaled the bleachers, and sat down beside her. "What are you doing here at this hour of the night?"

"I've been looking for you."

"Me?"

"*Where* have you been all evening?"

"Eddie and I had a couple of beers—"

"*I* wanted to talk to you," she interrupted. He

looked so appealingly boyish in his rumpled ball suit that she wanted to reach over and hug him until he made her stop. "Just look at you," she rebuked him.

Dex's gaze obediently went to the front of his dirty shirt.

"You haven't even cleaned up yet."

"Yeah, I know, but we weren't looking for women," he said as if that excused him.

Removing his hat, he ran his hands through his thick crop of hair. "What'd you want to talk to me about?"

The moonlight filtered softly down on the deserted bleachers, bathing the couple in silky mellow rays. Dex stretched his long legs out before him, relaxing.

"Well . . . I don't know where to begin," Carly admitted, her resolve not quite as strong now that they were alone, and she had his undivided attention.

"Let's see. Why don't you begin—say—a year ago," he suggested easily.

She glanced at him, realizing that *he* knew what she was about to say and was going to love watching her grovel.

"I—" She struggled to find the right words, Words had never come as easily to her as they did for him.

"I love you, Dex?" he supplied helpfully.

She lowered her eyes, gazing at the remains of the sticky, half-eaten Butterfinger. "Well . . . I do love you, Dex."

"I've always loved you, Dex, but for a while I was a little confused about what I wanted?" he offered. "Not that being confused occasionally is bad. I'm entitled to take my time about deciding who I want to spend my life with."

"I wasn't confused, Dex. I knew that I loved you. It was just . . . envy that made me break our engagement."

"Envy?"

"Yes, envy. You were always so darn good at everything. . . . I just began to feel inferior. Every day of my life, I felt more and inferior until I couldn't stand it any longer."

Leaning back, Dex studied the stars. "Yeah, I'm so darn good at everything. Look at my life. It's perfect. The woman I love broke her engagement to me, I moved to San Jose and was miserable as hell for a year, moved back to Chicago to prove to myself that I was no longer in love with the woman, and what happens? I discover I love her more than ever, but she can't love me back because I'm so perfect I make her feel inferior." He sighed. "My life couldn't be happier."

"I know it sounds ridiculous, but I've always had this inferiority complex a mile long. When you asked me out for the first time, I couldn't believe it. Here you were, drop-dead handsome, not to mention extremely talented, while I always have and probably always will be twenty pounds overweight and not exactly setting the world on fire."

Dex made a noise like a sigh, and Carly wasn't sure if it was from fatigue or impatience with her. "Those twenty pounds always bothered you a hell of a lot more than they bothered me."

"Of course, you would say that."

"Carly, I don't say what I don't mean," he said. "If I loved you for your looks alone, we wouldn't have a meaningful relationship. We would have an admiration society, and little else."

"But, Dex . . . you *are* so much more talented than me."

"Carly, you're looking at this the wrong way. I'm fairly good at my job, but you've got me beat all to hell when it comes to writing poetry or fixing a garage door or building mailboxes."

She couldn't help but grin. She *could* write a mean poem while he had trouble rhyming hat with cat. And he was *terrible* with power tools. She'd built two mailboxes and a wren house one afternoon while he was still trying to saw two boards evenly in half. "Or winning softball games?"

"Pure luck."

"Sore loser."

"You wait until next year. I'll have Edsel in marketing by then."

"You could have used Greta," she reminded him.

He wiggled his brows knowingly. "You said I couldn't."

"No—I don't mean that way. I meant you could

have had Greta pitch." Carly noticed that Greta had played right field most of the game.

"I didn't need a pitcher. I had one."

"Then you *really* didn't steal her from me, did you?"

"One more time—I transferred Greta to marketing because she was the best person for the job, nothing more, nothing less."

"Really?"

"Hello?" He reached over and knocked on her thick skull. "Anyone home? I didn't hire Greta because of the size of her bust—although Eddie and I agreed that we'll never be able to look at the Montrose O again in the same light—"

Carly whacked him across the knee.

"I didn't hire Greta just to steal your pitcher, and I didn't transfer Greta because I had the hots for her."

Carly smiled, leaning over to turn his face toward her. "Honestly?"

"Hello?" He knocked on her noggin again. "Anyone home?" His words were lost as Carly kissed him.

Dex drew her closer to him, and she sighed as she settled into his arms and his mouth closed hungrily over hers. This was how it should be. This was how she wanted it to be for the rest of their lives.

Arching against him, she kissed him deeply as his hands roamed over her body.

She could feel his need for her, and she desperately wanted things to be the way they once were.

"Dex." Her mouth moved from his, seeking the warm curve of his throat. If he wanted her to eat hippopotamus, she would. "Will you marry me? I made a mistake . . . I love you, and I'm sorry I broke our engagement."

"Carly . . ." Dex buried his face in the intoxicating scent of her hair.

"I'll . . . I'll lose weight, and I'll go back to school for my master's—you'll see. I can change, you'll see."

She felt him suddenly tense, and she hugged him tighter. "Dex?" she urged, knowing that she would surely die if he refused her.

"Ummm?"

"Will you marry me?"

"Unh-unh."

Lifting her eyes, her gaze met his disbelievingly. "No?"

He shook his head. "No can do."

"No can do?" she repeated lamely.

"Carly, we tried it once, and it didn't work. Maybe you should lose twenty pounds and get the master's, then we'll talk."

Words failed her as she just stared at him.

"Maybe in a couple of years, who knows?"

His words slammed into her stomach like a steel fist. "Dex . . . you can't be serious—" she protested. If this was his attempt at humor, it wasn't working.

But he was serious. Dead serious. "It won't work the way things are, Carly. Call me when you think you have everything in your life exactly the way you want it to be."

"But . . . I think we could make it work this time," she pleaded. "I can quit my job at Montrose and get another one so that we won't be competing with each other—and I can join a couple more aerobic classes. . . . A good marriage can be engineered just like any building. If two people love each other, they can build a solid foundation—"

Drawing her back to him quickly, he kissed her roughly, momentarily stilling her protests.

When they drew apart a few moments later, his gaze met hers in the soft moonlight. "Sorry, sweetheart, I honestly wish it could've worked."

"But . . . Dex—" The two Butterfingers rolled around in her stomach like sixteen-pound bowling balls.

Gently setting her aside, he stood up, stretched, then set his ball cap back on his head.

Turning back to her, he realized even in the dim light that her lower lip was trembling. "Hey, no hard feelings, tig?"

Shaking her head, Carly tried to swallow the golf-ball-size lump forming in her throat. "No," she murmured, "no hard feelings, Boomer."

She couldn't honestly say that she was surprised by his refusal, hurt, maybe, but not surprised. She hadn't really expected him to take her back.

"You'd better be getting home," he warned her, glancing at the deserted grounds. "It's not safe to be in the park at this hour of the night alone."

Scaling the fence again, he got back into his car. The window lowered on the passenger side, and he said quietly, "Go home, Carly."

Numb, Carly climbed off the bleachers and walked to her car. Dex waited until she drove out of the parking lot, then followed.

Go home, Carly. Dex's words echoed in her head as she pulled onto the freeway. *I'm sorry, but it won't work.* Nothing had changed. Clearly, he was telling her she was still a dork while he was a prince. Princes didn't marry dorks.

Carly felt her face burn with color. She had bared her soul to him—and he still didn't want her. Clearly, she wasn't good enough for him.

Mashing harder on the accelerator, she drove through the darkened streets, her stomach churning with resentment. She just wasn't good enough for him. He could say what he wanted, but that was the plain truth. Hey, no hard feelings, tig? He didn't have to spell it out in black and white. She wasn't dense. He wanted someone brighter, smarter, thinner.

She could see the headlights of his Corvette in the rearview mirror, and she drove faster.

He was probably having a good laugh at her expense. He was probably congratulating himself for the superb job he'd done rejecting her. He had surely shown her what an idiot she was for believing that she could cast aside a man like Dex and go unpunished. Oh, no, it wasn't over until *he* said it was over, and he'd clearly said it was. Good old Dex. When he did a job, he did it well.

Wheeling off the Dan Ryan Expressway, she glanced into the rearview mirror and saw that the Corvette was still following. She grew even more angry.

This wasn't his exit. Did he feel compelled to see her home safely so that she could die of a broken heart instead of a simple mugging?

As she swung down a side street, her anger suddenly consumed her. Jamming her foot on the brake, she brought her car to a dead stop in the middle of the quiet residential street.

Dex had to stand on his brakes to keep his Corvette from rear-ending the Camaro. In a squeal of burning rubber, he brought the car to a dead stop behind hers.

Slamming out of her car, Carly marched back to the Corvette. She might be a lot of things, but a doormat didn't happen to be one of them. If nothing else, she was going to have the satisfaction of telling him what a jerk he was.

Dex climbed out of his Corvette and leaned against it, bracing himself for her rage.

"*Nothing's* changed?" she challenged him. "Let me tell you something, Dex." She pointed her finger at him accusingly. "You're right! Nothing *has* changed, and it probably never will. I'm me, and you're you, and there's not a thing either one of us can do about it! Understand? Sure, I can beat my brains out trying to lose twenty pounds and *I could* go back and study for a master's degree that I really have no desire to achieve, *or* I can accept what I am and be happy—and *that's* exactly what I'm going to do—understand? I'm okay the way I am. I may not be the brightest person in the world, and I may not wear a size six—how many women do?—but I'll get by! And I'm going to *eat* a doughnut if I want one. Small children won't die from it! And I'll make mistakes, but I'll keep trying—and you know what? I may never eat another carton of low-fat yogurt as long as I live! From now on I refuse to worry about every single thing that I can't do as well as you. I *refuse* to compete with you or anyone else ever again." Throwing her arms wide, Carly turned her face skyward, drawing a deep, exhilarating breath. Free at last, free at last, great God almighty, she was free at last! "Carly Winters is who she is, world; either love her or get out of her face!"

A slow grin started at the corners of Dex's mouth.

"What are you laughing about?" she yelled. The man was driving her bananas! She was standing in the middle of the street at one o'clock in the morning, screaming like a lunatic, and he was just standing there, grinning at her.

"Well, it's about time."

"What does that mean? What are you criticizing about me now?"

"Time you realized that you are never going to be perfect in the eyes of the world, but, dammit, you're perfect for me. That's all that matters. Now ask me to marry you," he said.

Her breath caught, and tears welled in her eyes.

"Okay . . . marry me," she responded, "just the way I am—no miracles, no changes. Just me, Carly Winters."

"I'll marry you any day, anytime, anyplace, Carly Winters. No miracles, no changes." His eyes brimmed with love. Just for her.

"Oh, Dex." The anger drained from her and a sob tore from her throat as she flew into his arms. "Why do you do these things to me, you big lug?"

Closing his eyes, he held her tightly. "Because I love you, tig. Welcome home, baby. Don't ever leave me again. I don't think I'd make it a second time."

"But at the ball park—"

"I said what I said back at the ball park to wake you up. Hell, you're stronger than you think. I figured you would be ready to tear my head off by the time you'd gone two blocks. You made it three miles, sweetheart, so, see, you outdid me again. I wanted to stop you and tell you how much I loved you twenty feet out of the parking lot." Grasping her shoulders, he shook her gently, longing to kiss her, but, more important, wanting her to know that he loved her exactly as she was.

He wouldn't change a thing about her, and this time she was going to know it.

"You're a beautiful, gifted woman, Carly, and I love you so damn much, my teeth ache. But I don't want a relationship where we compete with each other. Carly Winters and Dex Matthews are a team. We complement each other. We're better when we're together than we could ever be apart.

We share the good times and the bad times, but we're always here for each other, That's the way it should be; that's the way it has to be."

"Oh, Dex, believe me, I've learned my lesson. You can go to Mexico and fight bulls buck naked if you want to, and I won't feel threatened. It won't bother me a bit," she vowed. "I'll come along and watch."

"It should be breathtaking."

"Sounds like it." She grinned, her heart about to burst with happiness.

Draping his arm around her neck, they began walking back to her car, their heads resting against each other. "You ever made love in the backseat of a Camaro with a buck-naked matador who would like to have the opportunity to show you how much he's missed you this past year?"

"Not that I can remember."

"You would surely remember something like that."

"I think so."

"Then how about letting a buck-naked, soon-to-be-husband advertising accountant make love to you in the backseat of a Camaro?" His eyes softened with love. "That poor jerk's missed you like hell."

Carly nodded. Tears of joy filled her eyes as their mouths drew together magnetically. It wasn't over between them. If they lived to be a hundred and two, it would never be over between them.

The new Carly Winters was absolutely sure of it.

Starting in February . . .

An exciting, unprecedented mass market publishing program designed just for you . . . and the way you buy books!

Over the past few years, the popularity of genre authors has been unprecedented. Their success is no accident, because readers like you demand high levels of quality from your authors and reward them with fierce loyalty.

Now Bantam Books, the foremost English language mass market publisher in the world, takes another giant step in leadership by dedicating the majority of its paperback list to six genre imprints each and every month.

The six imprints that you will see wherever books are sold are:

SPECTRA.

For five years the premier publisher of science fiction and fantasy. Now Spectra expands to add one title to its list each month, a horror novel.

CRIME LINE.

The award-winning imprint of crime and mystery fiction. Crime Line will expand to embrace even more areas of contemporary suspense.

DOMAIN.

An imprint that consolidates Bantam's dominance in the frontier fiction, historical saga, and traditional Western markets.

FALCON.

High-tech action, suspense, espionage, and adventure novels will all be found in the Falcon imprint, along with Bantam's successful Air & Space and War books.

BANTAM NONFICTION.

A wide variety of commercial nonfiction, including true crime, health and nutrition, sports, reference books . . . and much more

AND NOW IT IS OUR SPECIAL PLEASURE TO INTRODUCE TO YOU THE SIXTH IMPRINT

FANFARE

TM

FANFARE is the showcase for Bantam's popular women's fiction. With spectacular covers and even more spectacular stories. FANFARE presents three novels each month—ranging from historical to contemporary—all with great human emotion, all with great love stories at their heart, all by the finest authors writing in any genre.

FANFARE LAUNCHES IN FEBRUARY (on sale in early January) **WITH THREE BREATHTAKING NOVELS . . .**

THE WIND DANCER
by Iris Johansen

TEXAS! LUCKY
by Sandra Brown

WAITING WIVES
by Christina Harland

THE WIND DANCER.

From the spellbinding pen of Iris Johansen comes her most lush, dramatic, and emotionally touching romance yet—a magnificent historical about characters whose lives have been touched by the legendary Wind Dancer. A glorious antiquity, the Wind Dancer is a statue of a Pegasus that is encrusted with jewels . . . but whose worth is beyond the value of its precious stones, gold, and artistry. The Wind Dancer's origins are shrouded in the mist of time . . . and only a chosen few can unleash its mysterious powers. But WIND DANCER is, first and foremost, a magnificent love story. Set in Renaissance Italy where intrigues were as intricate as carved cathedral doors and affairs of state were ruled by affairs of the bedchamber. WIND DANCER tells the captivating story of the lovely and indomitable slave Sanchia and the man who bought her on a back street in Florence. Passionate, powerful *condottiere* Lionello Andreas would love Sanchia and endanger her with equal wild abandon as he sought to win back the prized possession of his family, the Wind Dancer.

TEXAS! LUCKY.

Turning her formidable talent for the first time to the creation of a trilogy, Sandra Brown gives readers a family to remember in the Tylers—brothers Lucky and Chase and their "little" sister Sage. In oil-bust country where Texas millionaires are becoming Texas panhandlers, the Tylers are struggling to keep their drilling business from bankruptcy. Each of the TEXAS! novels tells the love story of one member of the family and combines gritty and colorful characters with the fluid and sensual style the author is lauded for!

WAITING WIVES.
By marvelously talented newcomer Christina Harland, WAITING WIVES is the riveting tale of three vastly different women from different countries whose only bond is the fate of their men who are missing in Vietnam. In this unique novel of great human emotion, full of danger, bravery, and romance, Christina Harland brings to the written page what CHINA BEACH and TOUR OF DUTY have brought to television screens. This is a novel of triumph and honor and hope . . . and love.

Rave reviews are pouring in from critics and much-loved authors on FANFARE's novels for February—and for those in months to come. You'll be delighted and enthralled by works by Amanda Quick and Beverly Byrne, Roseanne Bittner and Kay Hooper, Susan Johnson and Nora Roberts . . . to mention only a few of the remarkable authors in the FANFARE imprint.

Special authors. Special covers. And very special stories.

Can you hear the flourish of trumpets now . . . the flourish of trumpets announcing that something special is coming?

FANFARE

Brief excerpts of the launch novels along with praise for them is on the following pages.

New York *Times* bestselling authors Catherine Coulter and Julie Garwood praise the advance copy they read of **WIND DANCER:**

"Iris Johansen is a bestselling author for the best of reasons—she's a wonderful storyteller. Sanchia, Lion, Lorenzo, and Caterina will wrap themselves around your heart and move right in. Enjoy, I did!"
—Catherine Coulter

"So compelling, so unforgettable a page-turner, this enthralling tale could have been written only by Iris Johansen. I never wanted to leave the world she created with Sanchia and Lion at its center."
—Julie Garwood

In the following brief excerpt you'll see why *Romantic Times* said this about Iris Johansen and **THE WIND DANCER:**

"The formidable talent of Iris Johansen blazes into incandescent brilliance in this highly original, mesmerizing love story."

We join the story as the evil Carpino, who runs a ring of prostitutes and thieves in Florence, is forcing the young heroine Sanchia to "audition" as a thief for the great *condottiere* Lionello, who waits in the piazza with his friend, Lorenzo, observing at a short distance.

"You're late!" Caprino jerked Sanchia into the shadows of the arcade surrounding the piazza.

"It couldn't be helped," Sanchia said breathlessly. "There was an accident . . . and we didn't get finished until the hour tolled . . . and then I had to wait until Giovanni left to take the—"

Caprino silenced the flow of words with an impatient motion of his hand. "There he is." He nodded across the crowded piazza. "The big man in the wine-colored velvet cape listening to the storyteller."

Sanchia's gaze followed Caprino's to the man standing in front of the platform. He was more than big, he was a giant, she thought gloomily. The careless arrogance in the man's stance bespoke perfect confidence in his ability to deal with any circumstances and, if he caught her, he'd probably use his big strong hands to crush her head like a walnut. Well, she was too tired to worry about that now. It had been over thirty hours since she had slept. Perhaps it was just as well she was almost too exhausted to care what happened to her. Fear must not make her as clumsy as she had been yesterday. She was at least glad the giant appeared able to afford to lose a few ducats. The richness of his clothing indicated he must either be a great lord or a prosperous merchant.

"Go." Caprino gave her a little push out onto the piazza. "Now."

She pulled her shawl over her head to shadow her face and hurried toward the platform where a man was telling a story, accompanying himself on the lyre.

A drop of rain struck her face, and she glanced up at the suddenly dark skies. Not yet, she thought with exasperation. If it started to rain in earnest the people crowding the piazza would run for shelter and she would have to follow the velvet-clad giant until he put himself into a situation that allowed her to make the snatch.

Another drop splashed her hand, and her anxious gaze flew to the giant. His attention was still fixed on the storyteller, but only the saints knew how long he would remain engrossed. This storyteller was not very good. Her pace quickened as she flowed like a shadow into the crowd surrounding the platform.

Garlic, Lion thought, as the odor assaulted his nostrils. Garlic, spoiled fish, and some other stench that smelled even fouler. He glanced around the crowd trying to identify the source of the smell. The people surrounding the platform were the same ones he had studied moments before, trying to search out Caprino's thief. The only new arrival was a thin woman dressed in a shabby gray gown, an equally ragged woolen shawl covering her head.

She moved away from the edge of the crowd and started to hurry across the piazza. The stench faded with her departure and Lion drew a deep breath. *Dio*, luck was with him in this, at least. He was not at all pleased at being forced to stand in the rain waiting for Caprino to produce his master thief.

"It's done," Lorenzo muttered, suddenly at Lion's side. He had been watching from the far side of the crowd. Now he said more loudly, "As sweet a snatch as I've ever seen."

"What?" Frowning, Lion gazed at him. "There was no—" He broke off as he glanced down at his belt. The pouch was gone; only the severed cords remained in his belt. "Sweet Jesus." His gaze flew around the piazza. "Who?"

"The sweet madonna who looked like a beggar maid and smelled like a decaying corpse." Lorenzo nodded toward the arched arcade. "She disappeared behind that column, and I'll wager you'll find Caprino lurking there with her, counting your ducats."

Lion started toward the column. "A woman," he murmured. "I didn't expect a woman. How good is she?"

Lorenzo fell into step with him. "Very good."

Iris Johansen's fabulous romances of characters whose lives are touched by the Wind Dancer go on! STORM WINDS, coming from FANFARE in June 1991, is another historical. REAP THE WIND, a contemporary, will be published by FANFARE in November 1991.

Sandra Brown, whose legion of fans catapulted her last contemporary novel onto the *New York Times* list, has received the highest praise in advance reviews of **TEXAS! LUCKY**. *Rave Reviews* said, "Romance fans will relish all of Ms. Brown's provocative sensuality along with a fast-paced plotline that springs one surprise after another. Another feast for the senses from one of the world's hottest pens."

Indeed Sandra's pen is "hot"—especially so in her incredible **TEXAS!** trilogy. We're going to peek in on an early episode in which Lucky has been hurt in a brawl in a bar where he was warding off the attentions of two town bullies toward a redhead he hadn't met, but wanted to get to know very well.

This woman was going to be an exciting challenge, something rare that didn't come along every day. Hell, he'd never had anybody exactly like her.

"What's your name?"

She raised deep forest-green eyes to his. "D-D Dovey."

" 'D-D Dovey'?"

"That's right," she snapped defensively. "What's wrong with it?"

"Nothing. I just hadn't noticed your stuttering before. Or has the sight of my bare chest made you develop a speech impediment?"

"Hardly. Mr.—?"

"Lucky."

"Mr. Lucky?"

"No, I'm Lucky."

"Why is that?"

"I mean my name is Lucky. Lucky Tyler."

"Oh. Well. I assure you the sight of your bare chest leaves me cold, Mr. Tyler."

He didn't believe her and the smile that tilted up one corner of his mouth said so. "Call me Lucky."

She reached for the bottle of whiskey on the nightstand and raised it in salute. "Well, Lucky, your luck just ran out."

"Huh?"

"Hold your breath." Before he could draw a sufficient one, she tipped the bottle and drizzled the liquor over the cut.

He blasted the four walls with words unfit to be spoken aloud, much less shouted. "Oh hell, oh—"

"Your language isn't becoming to a gentleman, Mr. Tyler."

"I'm gonna murder you. Stop pouring that stuff— Agh!"

"You're acting like a big baby."

"What the hell are you trying to do, scald me?"

"Kill the germs."

"Damn! It's killing *me*. Do something. Blow on it."

"That only causes germs to spread."

"Blow on it!"

She bent her head over his middle and blew gently along the cut. Her breath fanned his skin and cooled the stinging whiskey in the open wound. Droplets of it had collected in the satiny stripe of hair beneath his navel. Rivulets trickled beneath the waistband of his jeans. She blotted at them with her fingertips, then, without thinking, licked the liquor off her own skin. When she realized what she'd done, she sprang upright. "Better now?" she asked huskily.

When Lucky's blue eyes connected with hers, it was like completing an electric circuit. The atmosphere crackled. Matching her husky tone of voice, he said, "Yeah, much better. . . . Thanks," he mumbled. Her hand felt so comforting and cool, the way his mother's always had whenever he was sick with fever. He captured Dovey's hand with his and pressed it against his hot cheek.

She withdrew it and, in a schoolmarm's voice, said, "You can stay only until the swelling goes down."

"I don't think I'll be going anywhere a-tall tonight," he said. "I feel like hell. This is all I want to do. Lie here. Real still and quiet."

Through a mist of pain, he watched her remove her jacket and drape it over the back of a chair. Just as he'd thought—quite a looker was Dovey. But that wasn't all. She looked like a woman who knew her own mind and wasn't afraid to speak it. Levelheaded.

So what the hell had she been doing in that bar? He drifted off while puzzling through the question.

Now on sale in DOUBLEDAY hardcover is the next in Sandra's fantastic trilogy, TEXAS! CHASE, about which *Rendezvous* has said: ". . . it's the story of a love that is deeper than the oceans, and more lasting than the land itself. Lucky's story was fantastic; Chase's story is more so." FANFARE's paperback of TEXAS! CHASE will go on sale August 1991.

Rather than excerpt from the extraordinary novel **WAITING WIVES**, which focuses on three magnificent women, we will describe the book in some detail. The three heroines whom you'll love and root for give added definition to the words growth and courage . . . and love.

ABBRA is talented and sheltered, a raven-haired beauty who was just eighteen when she fell rapturously in love with handsome Army captain Lewis Ellis. Immediately after their marriage he leaves for Vietnam. Passionately devoted to Lewis, she lives for his return—until she's told he's dead. Then her despair turns to torment as she falls hopelessly in love with Lewis's irresistible brother. . . .

SERENA never regrets her wildly impulsive marriage to seductive Kyle Anderson. But she does regret her life of unabashed decadence and uninhibited pleasure—especially when she discovers a dirty, bug-infested orphanage in Saigon . . . and Kyle's illegitimate child.

GABRIELLE is the daughter of a French father and a Vietnamese mother. A flame-haired singer with urchin appeal and a sultry voice, she is destined for stardom. But she gives her heart—and a great part of her future—to a handsome Aussie war correspondent. Gavin is determined to record the "real" events of the Vietnam war . . . but his search for truth leads him straight into the hands of the Viet Cong and North Vietnamese, who have no intention of letting him report anything until they've won the war.

Christina Harland is an author we believe in. Her story is one that made all of us who work on FANFARE cry, laugh, and turn pages like mad. We predict that WAITING WIVES will fascinate and enthrall you . . . and that you will say with us, "it is a novel whose time has come."

We hope you will greet FANFARE next month with jubilation! It is an imprint we believe you will delight in month after month, year after year to come.

THE EDITOR'S CORNER

What could be more romantic—Valentine's Day and six LOVESWEPT romances all in one glorious month. And I have the great pleasure of writing my first editor's corner. Let me introduce myself: My name is Nita Taublib, and I have worked as an editorial consultant with the Loveswept staff since Loveswept began. As Carolyn is on vacation and Susann is still at home with her darling baby daughter, I have the honor of introducing the fabulous reading treasures we have in store for you. February is a super month for LOVESWEPT!

Deborah Smith's heroes are always fascinating, and in **THE SILVER FOX AND THE RED-HOT DOVE,** LOVESWEPT #450, the mysterious T. S. Audubon is no exception. He is intrigued by the shy Russian woman who accompanies a famous scientist to a party. And he finds himself filled with a desire to help her escape from her keepers! But when Elena Petrovic makes her own desperate escape, she is too terrified to trust him. Could her handsome enigmatic white-haired rescuer be the silver fox of her childhood fantasy, the only man who could set her loose from a hideous captivity, or does he plan to keep her for himself? Mystery and romance are combined in this passionate tale that will move you to tears.

What man could resist having a gorgeous woman as a bodyguard? Well, as Gail Douglas shows in **BANNED IN BOSTON,** LOVESWEPT #451, rugged and powerful Matt Harper never expects a woman to show up when his mother hires a security consultant to protect him after he receives a series of threatening letters. Annie Brentwood is determined to prove that the best protection de-

(continued)

mands brains, not brawn. But she forgets that she must also protect herself from the shameless, arrogant, and oh-so-male Matt, who finds himself intoxicated and intrigued by her feisty spirit. Annie finds it hard to resist a man who promises her the last word and I guarantee you will find this a hard book to put down.

Patt Bucheister's hero in **TROPICAL STORM**, LOVESWEPT #452, will make your temperature rise to sultry heights as he tries to woo Cass Mason. Wyatt Brodie has vowed to take Cass back to Key West for a reconciliation with her desperately ill mother. He challenges her to face her past, promising to help if she'll let him. Can she dare surrender to the hunger he has ignited in her yearning heart? Wyatt has warned her that once he makes love to her, they can never be just friends, that he'll fight to keep her from leaving the island. Can he claim the woman he's branded with the fire of his need? Don't miss this very touching, very emotional story.

From the sunny, sultry South we move to snowy Denver in **FROM THIS DAY FORWARD**, LOVESWEPT #453, by Joan Elliot Pickart. John-Trevor Payton has been assigned to befriend Paisley Kane to discover if sudden wealth and a reunion with the father she's never known will bring her happiness or despair. When Paisley knocks John-Trevor into a snowdrift and falls into his arms, his once firmly frozen plans for eternal bachelorhood begin to melt. Paisley has surrounded herself with a patchwork family of nutty boarders in her Denver house, and John-Trevor envies the pleasure she gets from the people she cares for. But Paisley fears she must choose between a fortune and the man destined to

(continued)

be hers. Don't miss this wonderful romance—a real treat for the senses!

Helen Mittermeyer weaves another fascinating story of two lovers reunited in **THE MASK**, LOVE-SWEPT #455. When Cas Griffith lost his young bride to a plane crash over Nepal he was full of grief and guilt and anger. He believed he'd never again want a woman as he'd desired Margo, but when he comes face-to-face with the exotic, mysterious T'ang Qi in front of a New York art gallery two years later, he feels his body come to life again— and knows he must possess the artist who seems such an unusual combination of East and West. The reborn love discovered through their suddenly intimate embraces stuns them both as they seek to exorcise the ghosts of past heartbreak with a love that knows the true meaning of forever.

Sandra Chastain's stories fairly sizzle with powerful emotion and true love, and for this reason we are thrilled to bring you **DANNY'S GIRL**, LOVE-SWEPT #454. Katherine Sinclair had found it hard to resist the seductive claim Danny Dark's words had made on her heart when she was seventeen. Danny had promised to meet her after graduation, but he never came, leaving her to face a pregnancy alone. She'd given the baby up for adoption, gone to college, ended up mayor of Dark River, and never heard from Danny again . . . until now. Has he somehow discovered that she was raising her son, Mike—their son—now that his adoptive parents had died? Has he returned merely to try to take Mike from her? Danny still makes her burn and ache with a sizzling passion, but once they know the truth about the past, they have to discover if it is love or only memory that has lasted.

(continued)

Katherine longs to show him that they are a family, that the only time she'll ever be happy is in his arms. You won't soon forget this story of two people and their son trying to become a family.

I hope that you enjoy each and every one of these Valentine treats. We've got a great year of reading pleasure in store for you. . . .

Sincerely,

Nita Taublib

Nita Taublib,
Editorial Consultant,
LOVESWEPT
Bantam Books
666 Fifth Avenue
New York, NY 10103

THE "VIVE LA ROMANCE" SWEEPSTAKES

Don't miss your chance to speak to your favorite Loveswept authors on the LOVESWEPT LINE 1-900-896-2505*

You may win a glorious week for two in the world's most romantic city, Paris, France by entering the "Vive La Romance" sweepstakes when you call. With travel arrangements made by Reliable Travel, you and that special someone will fly American Airlines to Paris, where you'll be guests at the famous Lancaster Hotel. Why not call right now? Your own Loveswept fantasy could come true!

Official Rules:

Official Rules cont'd

2. 1 Grand Prize: A vacation trip for two to Paris, France for 7 nights. Trip includes accommodations at the deluxe Lancaster Hotel and round-trip coach tickets to Paris on American Airlines from the American Airlines airport nearest the winner's residence which provides direct service to New York.
(Approximate Retail Value: $3,500).

3. Sweepstakes begins October 1, 1990 and all entries must be received by December 31, 1990. All entrants must be 18 years of age or older at the time of entry. The winner will be chosen by Bantam's Marketing Department by a random drawing to be held on or about January 15, 1991 from all entries received and will be notified by mail. Bantam's decision is final. The winner has 30 days from date of notice in which to accept the prize award or an alternate winner will be chosen. The prize is not transferable and no substitution is allowed. The trip must be taken by November 22, 1991, and is subject to airline departure schedules and ticket and accommodation availability. Certain blackout periods may apply. Winner must have a valid passport. Odds of winning depend on the number of entries received. Enter as often as you wish, but each mail-in entry must be entered separately. No mechanically reproduced entries allowed.

4. The winner and his or her guest will be required to execute an Affidavit of Eligibility and Promotional Release supplied by Bantam. Entering the sweepstakes constitutes permission for use of winner's name, address and likeness for publicity and promotional purposes, with no additional compensation or permission.

5. This sweepstakes is open only to residents of the U.S. who are 18 years of age or older, and is void in Puerto Rico and wherever else prohibited or restricted by law. Employees of Bantam Books, Bantam Doubleday Dell Publishing Group, Inc., Reliable Travel, Call Interactive, their subsidiaries and affiliates, and their immediate family members are not eligible to enter this sweepstakes. Taxes, if any, are the winner's sole responsibility.

6. Bantam is the sole sponsor of the sweepstakes. Bantam reserves the right to cancel the sweepstakes via the 900 number at any time and without prior notice, but entry into the sweepstakes via mail through December 31, 1990 will remain. Bantam is not responsible for lost, delayed or misdirected entries, and Bantam, Call Interactive, and AT&T are not responsible for any error, incorrect or inaccurate entry of information by entrants, malfunctions of the telephone network, computer equipment software or any combination thereof. This Sweepstakes is subject to the complete Official Rules.

7. For the name of the prize winner (available after January 15, 1991), send a stamped, self-addressed envelope entirely separate from your entry to:

VIVE LA ROMANCE SWEEPSTAKES WINNER LIST,
Bantam Books, Dept. CK-3, 666 Fifth Avenue,
New York, New York 10103.

Loveswept ®